SYDNEY'S CONVICTS

Logan Firth

Inspiring Publishers
P.O. Box 159, Calwell, ACT Australia 2905
Email: publishaspg@gmail.com
http://www.inspiringpublishers.com

A catalogue record for this book is available from the National Library of Australia

National Library of Australia The Prepublication Data Service

Author: Logan Firth
Title: Sydney's Convicts
Genre: Fiction

Paperback ISBN: 978-0-646-71118-8

Author's Preface

My dear fellow Australians, here we are as the nation of Australia. Our nation's story is unique. We went from being a penal colony, to a country of many outstanding achievements. Past or present, our story couldn't be achieved without the initiative and courage of our people. From the convicts to now, we have truly come from everywhere on this earth. We have left all that is dear to us. We have come together across the seas to build our nation. Those people have proudly, and continue to, represent Australia and her people.

This all starts with our Indigenous Australians. For 65,000 years they lived on this land and off its resources. Then in 1788, the white colonists came to launch Australia through the violence, massacres, dispossession, assimilation, and segregation of their Indigenous population. A population, who had faithfully spilled their blood in the defence of their countries. Throughout my childhood, their stories have always fascinated me. It even inspired me to start researching the history of my own ancestors.

It amazes me to think of how we went from a penal colony to an outstanding nation. It fascinated me to think of the people behind this; the convicts, the settlers, the explorers, the drovers, the ordinary, the children, the young people, the disadvantaged, and so forth. These past people, today's ordinary, and First Nation Australians, are truly our Australian pioneers. Their perspectives and patriotism has ignited my Australianness. It has sparked my hidden love for our bush. Forever, I proudly identify as an Australian at soul and heart.

I forever swear my defence and loyalty to my motherland. Now, having researched the story of our nation through mainstream eyes; I take on another approach. I feel it my duty to do so as an Australian historical writer. I will re-write our nation's history through three major perspectives; the Indigenous Australians, the white people, and those who came by sea. This vision starts with our first colonists and First Nation Australians.

This book is about a girl's endurance, hope, trauma, romantic love, and sufferings. It is about her experiences, witnesses, of the internal battles in the struggle to birth New South Wales. It starts with the tragedy of her own battle for survival that resulted in conviction. It then ends in her new freedom in an expanding colony. Her story is a representation of one of the more than 162,000 convicts transported to Australia. Do note, this is not a true based story. Only its historical contents and noteable background characters are real. Rather, it is a voice to the convicts, the free colonists, and the Indigenous Australians.

Yet, not all Australians today are ready to embrace their convict ancestors. Today, one in every 5 Australians bear convicted ancestors. No matter their convicted crime, only love and pride for them breathes. We ought to assimilate all shame surrounding our convict strain. Instead, we shall let further understanding of these past people brighten our Australianness.

Thus, I dedicate this book to all the convicts who were transported here. By writing this story, I hope my fellow Australians will lose the last shame around convict pride. I hope their better understanding and emotional connection will lead to this outcome. Last of all, I dedicate it to my convict ancestors, so a light may be shed on their stories. Very last of all, I dedicate this book to my family and mates who have always supported and loved me.

Now, I leave it to you to forge a better understanding. May that understanding kindle the true love and pride for our convict ancestors. I wish you all the best, my dear fellow Australians.

Logan Firth (author), Canberra, Australia
January 2025.

CHAPTER 1

December 31st, 1787.

Dawn arises; its reflective golden rays endorsing the shiny calm golden ocean. Seagulls cry out to each other. They chase each other with confidence through the dazzling fleet of ships. The fleet of eleven ships proudly bear the following names: Charlotte, Scarborough, Prince of Wales, Lady Penrhyd, Friendship, Borrowdale, Golden Grove, HMS Sirius, Fishburn, HMAS Supply and Alexander.

A British flag attached to a mast pole lazily flapped in the breeze. An explorer by the name of Captain Arthur Phillip gazed at the flag. He smiled at the thought of cleansing Britain of her unwanted felons. Too many thought themselves good enough to turn their back against Britain's goodness and commit such theft. *And what good was there in her?* They had snarled. *Factories and mines are taking our generation's old way of labours. It's installing the fever and itchiness to abandon the countryside to the smoke-filled cities and towns. It's leaving us poor in the greediness of our upper citizens. What more were we to do?* They angrily spat in their bitterness.

Such an excuse, hear it all the time, the bored constables had thought. *Stuffing yourself with ill-gotten goods for your skinny and starving physiques doesn't make the cut,* they had retorted. As Britain's jails filled with these unwanted felons, she had itched to remove them. But to where? The damn Yankees had become enraged by British treatment toward them. Thus, they determinedly spilled their blood for complete independence and freedom. They left a shamed Britain to bitterly cry and retreat from the world stage temporarily. Of course, the Yankees wouldn't want the felons anymore, but it wouldn't come to matter anyway.

Captain James Cook had discovered and wrote and talked of this great South Land at the bottom of the world. He had talked of great rock formations, hulking rock cliffs, tall sprawling leafy gum trees, furry creatures, hard dry land and Indigenous people partly-covered. He had even noted their wooden gear. He had been greeted by a swarm of these tall and healthy people. Little did he know, they were the proud First Nation Australians.

One day, Phillip was approached and informed he was to lead a fleet to this unknown land to start a British civilisation there. He had many mixed emotions in such little time. He couldn't give it much thought, until the day the fleet left grey London behind in the breeze. It was May 1787 when the fleet departed.

Now, he stood staring at the British flag that had picked up its pace. The breeze gently fluttered his black uniform long coat. The sun made the golden buttons shine. His distinctive, angular shoulder-shaped governor's hat, held his wig firmly against the breeze. His white long-sleeved top, breeches, stockings and brown shoulders completed his splendid appearance.

The marines, wives, children and crew lavished in the morning sun without unmoving Phillip. Meanwhile, convicts moaned awake in the pitch-dark covered lower decks. They had been rowed in boats, then boarded into those decks, where it was overcrowded. Only one didn't awaken. 12-year-old Emily Wilson. Thin-railed, wavy brown hair that reached her hips, amber eyes and freckles covering her nose and hollow cheeks. Her complexion as white as a ghost. The girl rolled to the other side. Her brown petticoat and her white stockings were faded, ripped, torn and stained. Murmuring she was, the childhood scars of the past she was fast leaving. A past of scars her resemblance bore. She had been poor all her childhood.

Before this industrial revolution gripped Britain, Emily ran rampant through the green fields of the Wilsons' countryside farm. She had experienced freedom in the games she played and the creatures she spent time with. But she was too young to feel that freedom. Her severely ill, loving father had perished when she was 7. Illness and death had at long last relieved him to God; to heaven. Then suddenly they had become bitterly poor, her mother's pained tears telling their outcome. Emily's very feet had helped to move furniture, sell it, and put their very few possessions on the carriage to London.

How she had withered at the majestic buildings; how she had coughed at the bleak smoke ever since. How she had cried, anguished, from exhaustion and the loss of her father in the strong arms of her grandmother. How the Industrial Revolution had forced her mother and her to labour barefoot in the factories Emily despised. How their wage left them poor and fighting for survival. The then-12-year-old Emily Wilson gave way to her misery and starvation, allowing it to make her a cunning thief.

Banding with other local kids, they stole whatever survival goods they could put their fingers on. But she was caught. She was thrown into Newgate Prison, as a screaming, crying felon. The stink, the loneliness, the harassment, the overcrowding, the poor diet, the sharp frigid, blistering heat, diseases, drunkenness, executions, tortures, hanging, insanity and chains are not enough to describe the hell of Newgate Prison. She lost count of the bouts of sickness she suffered. A hell that grief-sicked Emily wished to die in. But yet, the memory of her two living loved ones, her deceased father and hope got her through.

Yet, when she felt the heavy weight of chains drag all of the convicts into the hulls, then onto the fleet's ships, her true hell had only just arrived. Now here they are, crossing endless oceans and waves. London had become a far memory. Now she has lost count in this endless darkness. The convicts knew little of sunlight. Days were spent below the wooden decks, in wooden bunks. Only an hour per day were they permitted on deck, in chains, for sunlight. The iron buckets carried the stench of the detested human waste that sometimes overflowed. The starvation gnawed at their physically awful, diseased and malnourished bodies. The strong, healthy bodies of the fleet's non-felons angrily envied the convicts. The bodies of the convicts too raged with dysentery, cholera and sexually-transmitted diseases.

Emily would hear the raging curses and foul tongues of the victims. The worst cry of all was the women wailing at the losses of their babies and children. It would make Emily want to cry with memories and grief. At night, they would tie themselves to the wooden bunks; any curse and a thud, Emily would know someone had fallen off. Severe storms meant the worst sleep, they forced you to fight to stay on your bed as you were tumbled about. *Perhaps the ship dislikes curses*, Emily would ponder.

One of the only two pleasures the convicts yearned for in the journey's duration was solid land without the damned chains. It came at their first stop, Cruz Tenerife, Spain (June 3rd - June 10, 1787). Captain Arthur Phillip and the crew loaded the fresh water onto the ships. Meanwhile the convicts rejoiced in their pleasure. The captain next hoped to stop off at Port Praia for much-wanted supplies.

However, his hopes were dashed upon missing the port. The convicts were to experience a second pleasure of solid land. This came when the fleet anchored at Rio de Janeiro, Brazil (August 6th- September, 1787). The condition of her body, and the toll of the journey, at last bode Emily to illness. Reeled by her humid body stench, a marine's wife gave her a dress and a good wash. Emily didn't miss the convict's miseries, she lavished in the fresh cool water to drink and a proper bed to lay in. Once recovered, Emily joined the convicts in time to be put in a better health condition. The convicts were fed daily food rations and a quantity of oranges. However, Emily found her body reeled at the introduction of such regular food. Thus she could only take a very small amount of the nourishment. The fleet purchased sheep and plants. At last, the fleet left the bay on November 12th, 1787, to this strange land.

Suddenly, Emily felt her petticoats being ruffled. She cracked an eye open and gasped. Coming to her senses, she rolled over and landed with a thud. Wincing, Emily sprung to her feet and hugged the wooden wall.

"Sorry Miss, I wanted a child," said the man.

Just like all convict men, he was dressed in stockings, woollen drawers, breeches, a waistcoat, a shirt and a jacket. His clothes were just as rugged, stained, ripped and worn.

"Don't worry Miss, just another one of those, it was," reassured a woman behind her.

Nodding, Emily fell to the floor. She retreated a little more from the amused convict man. Closing her eyes, she hugged the wooden wall. For no longer could the loving arms of her mother provide comfort. Meanwhile, her ears heard the slurps of convicts drinking from iron buckets of water. It also heard others eating the crumbs of little nourishment the crew threw down to them.

CHAPTER 2

Lost in the darkness and disillusioned by the convict's journey she had endured, Emily lost track of the days. Cold and starving, Emily felt weakened beyond words by the fever. A fever that laid her down on the hard, wooden floor. She wanted to be relieved to the eternal life of Heaven. Something only death could relieve her to. But it was as if God couldn't bear to abruptly end her misery in that manner. Voices and movement above the deck just barely kept her awake.

The manhole opened, the convicts reeling from the bright sunlight. Their shaking hands shaded their eyes.

"Get out, you felons," harshly ordered the marines.

Emily failed to move, her eyes watched the convicts who had endured the journey with her. They were moving like ghosts up the sunlit ladder. She heard the thud of those who simply fell, withering and sapped of strength. Pain and understanding stabbed her, as no one went to help her. They instead helped the weakened, older and much younger convicts.

Emily closed her eyes in desperation to forget, as well as dream of the life she could have had. She felt the bitter tears sting her delicate flesh. At last, Emily remained the last convict on board.

"Oi girlie, what are you doing? Get out!" commanded the marines.

"Excuse me, may I see her?" a marine's wife asked.

"I suppose so," they gruffly agreed, and moved aside.

Climbing down the ladder, and appearing by the girl's side, Emily cried harder at the sight of kindness. Her blurred vision soaked in the lady's features. She saw silky brown hair tied into a tight bun. Rosy cheeks adorned the relatively pale complexion. Blue eyes looked down a straight nose.

"My dear, just how sick, malnourished and delicate you are!" she remarked.

Emily burst into loud and gulping miserable sobs.

"My name is Elizabeth, and you?" the lady asked.

"Emily Wilson," said Emily.

"Let me help you, dear," said Elizabeth.

She gently lifted Emily into her arms. Emily's voice returned with screams of pain. Her joints cracked after days in a static position. She was helped up the ladder and into the sunlight London hadn't made her immune to. Screaming, Emily reeled and weakly shielded her eyes. Reassuring the girl, Elizabeth brought Emily ashore and laid her in the water's cool current. Elizabeth hurried to fetch Surgeon White.

Emily turned to her side, the wet sand buried underneath her. She saw the crew starting to unload the supplies, and the marines directing the throes of convicts. She saw them in the small clearing with this flapping British flag that Phillip's crew had previously pitched. She could already see erected tents bustling with activity.

It was January 27th, 1788. Emily and other convicts were brought to the shores of Sydney Cove. Only the crew had the first pleasures of coming to the shores on January 26th, 1788. Now here she was laid on those very shores, in cool ocean water for the first time. Curling into a protective ball, Emily shivered as Elizabeth approached with Surgeon White.

"I'm afraid I'm at full capacity," Surgeon White gazed mournfully at the girl.

"I understand," Elizabeth gathered Emily into her arms.

"What is she doing here?" demanded Elizabeth's husband, the tall and handsome James behind her. Emily turned to face the intruder. She saw brown hair neatly brushed to his side. A serious gaze lighted his brown eyes. Just like his wife, his complexion was white.

"Oh James, she is too sick to be with the others," said Elizabeth.

"She is a convict and a thief, she only belongs with the other felons," said James with vitriol.

"I stole for survival!" weakly protested Emily.

"What an excuse, I hear it all the time," retorted James.

"Please, let me take care of her until she's well again. I'll keep her out of your hair," pleaded Elizabeth.

Emily flinched as Elizabeth hugged her close.

"Fine," huffed James, swiftly departing.

"I'm sorry, your appearance reminds him of our daughter's death. He was very close to her. He hasn't been himself since then."

Emily silently nodded, too exhausted to speak again.

Emily gazed out to the ocean, the sunset turning the ocean to a reflective pool of purple and golden shades. The seagulls called out to each other. The waves lapped against the hem of her dress. She felt despair, lost and lonely in this unfamiliar land. So far she was, yet so close in memories to her loved ones in bustling London. It hurt her heart, stung it so strongly, pained it so strongly, saddened it so strongly, to feel that closeness. It made her hands clench tightly and her bitter tears stain her deathly pale complexion.

She felt Britain would forget her fleet and new colony. She felt being forgotten would lead the convicts to rot in starvation. Then for death to gladly relieve them each to Heaven, if there was any. The barren strangeness of this land; just how were they meant to birth a new civilisation in this dryness and blitzing heat? How was a city meant to spring up in Sydney Cove in this condition? This dry, dusty, sprawling land; just how were their malfunctioned hearts meant to breed the love for their new home? When here they had been transported as punished or exiled souls. The rolling green fields of their native Britain, now a distant reality, were never to be seen again by many of the transportees. However, forever were their hearts to truly regard the land of their miseries, Britain, their home. Emily closed her eyes and fell asleep in Elizabeth's arms, her thoughts silenced.

CHAPTER 3

Three days later arrived. Laying awake, Emily's ears heard the unfamiliarity, caused by the weird birds, the thud of the rat-looking furballs bounding along and the singing of the crickets. She didn't like the frown of the silent-watching magpies and kookaburras. Curling herself into a ball and bringing the blanket to her chin, Emily glanced at the sleeping Elizabeth. James must have departed early to whatever marine duty awaited him.

Turning around, Emily gasped and scrambled to her feet. A youth's face, paled and dishevelled, stared back. Emily blinked furiously; she ought to be dreaming. Convict children wouldn't be allowed to freely roam about, would they? Bracing the pain, Emily dragged herself and half-ran after that figure. But she collapsed on the hard-earth floor, spitting dirt from her mouth. Gritting her teeth, Emily dragged herself along the terrain. The sticks gashed her flesh, the dress soaked in her dark blood.

The figure seemed to endlessly bound ahead of her, glancing behind every now and then. The land coming to an end, Emily thought the figure would pause. Instead, she saw them leap. Faithful they were that they would find their grip on the rock wall. Screaming and still weak by the fever, Emily outstretched her arms. Her fingers reached for what wasn't there.

Dragging herself to the edge, Emily frantically searched the rocks. Itching further forward, she looked further over the edge. Suddenly, hands grabbed her and Emily rolled over. She felt nothing but air, as she plummeted towards the ocean water of Sydney Cove. Voices rung out, drowned by the water enveloping her. Turning and twisting, she felt her strength leaving. She opened her mouth to scream for help, but instead she violently shook, her arms and legs floundering in the tide. She felt water splash against her body and lay her down. The water seemed to pull her downwards, gurgling bubbles escaping her mouth and floating to the surface. Her vision went black as she shook one last time.

But that mysterious figure hadn't perished. They swam towards her. They wrapped their arms around Emily's waist, bringing her to shore. They laid the unmoving girl on the sand. After some time, Emily reeled and coughed up mouthfuls of ocean liquid. Hurried footsteps approached, and the figure ran into the heavy bush. There, they silently observed.

"Oh Emily," gasped Elizabeth.

"Bring her to my tent," ordered Surgeon White.

Emily stared into the thick bush surrounding James' property. Ever since her underwater seizure, Elizabeth had feared the recovering girl going to the ocean alone. Furthermore, she believed the fever was giving Emily hallucinations following her explanation of the mysterious figure. But Emily knew the figure was just as real as her. Her ears perked up at the nearby scratching. Looking around her, she snatched the nearest stick and held it before her. Dropping low, she ignored the exhaustion from her fever, instead sneaking forward. Gripping the stick more firmly, Emily levelled it up. A furry creature with a bushy tail and glassy eyes. Thwacking the stick down nearby caused the creature to shriek and run.

Emily threw herself forward, the creature darting underneath her. She landed in a *Phacelia sericea* bush. Screaming as what felt like a thousand knives stabbed her, she tried heaving herself out. Biting her tongue, she grimly allowed the thorns to rip her flesh. The blood gushed from the deep cuts on her skin. Freeing herself, Emily saw the mysterious figure approach her. She froze and observed the figure. She saw green eyes, long silky brown hair and many freckles. Emily believed the tall and lanky girl to be Irish.

"I'm sorry I scared you," came the round sound of the Irish accent.

"As if I ain't seeing strangers every day," replied Emily, crossing her arms.

"Off that horde, I guess?"

"What?"

"Off that horde, that came in about three days ago?"

"Oh, us felons and 'em crew. Yes."

"I thought so! That's how the flaming hell we got here."

"What do you mean, aren't you one of them?"

"Before I was, but now I have defected."

"Then who are you, and how did you get here?"

Rolling her head back, the tall and lanky skinny figure laughed. She answered in the same accent.

"I was one of youse felons. A severe illness passed through my family. It sapped their strength, till the Lord relieved them in death's darkness. I became one of those lost souls; roaming the streets free with the children and stealing survival goods. Of course , I was thrown in gaol then shipped to Britain for transportation."

"I despised the sufferings of starvation, cold, heat, abuse, and neglect that made gaol my home. Many times I longed to be dead. Many times I wished I wasn't in existence. Then rowed I was, to the cradle of my darkness at sea. Upon landing here, I snuck off into the unfamiliarity."

Here the Irish girl gathered her breath before continuing her narration. "I came across the First Inhabitants. They took me as one of theirs and passed to me the strength of their ways. They taught me their language, so I may speak with their clan. With a compassionate nurturing of a land and the life that breathes within it, I will be provided for in return. This wisdom is a sacred knowledge of their ancestor's understanding. It passes to their elders, who then exchange it with their people. That wisdom has blossomed in me a love for the rough beauty of this land."

"The art of carefully hunting mammals, birds, fish, and reptiles was passed to me. Nourishment, but also medicine, were sustained by the wealth of the bush fauna. Their interpretation of the world, the messages perceived by their lifestyle, and their connection to land echoed through their art. Art, embedded into gathered natural resources surrounding their home."

"The sense of belonging was strong, thriving, as were their connection to land and people. This was expressed through ceremony, song, dance, and welcoming of newborns. Most powerful of all, was the unification of tribes in and beyond this cove in those moments. These different tribes, whose vocals uttered different dialects, were also gathered by the message sticks. Survival and hunting tools were also naturally made. Controlled burning prevents severe fires and encourages regrowth of the ecosystem."

"Now, this world of peace, and living alongside nature, is fast slipping from reality. For, in the glory of Britain and her queen, you colonists are destroying it. Depriving your people of these natives from connection to country and environment. Degrading, are your ways on their lifestyle and manners of survival."

"How the construction of this colony is ripping them of their access to nourishment, medicine, and water. How their blood leaks and stains the terrain, as white hands massacre, poison, and beat them up. Then how those abusers push, shove them, into exile of unfamiliar lands. Thus, the natives destroy, kidnap, and wound your people in resistance to your oppression."

"But, we can show the righteous by defending their blood and stance against colonists brutality. But blame you I don't, as I know you don't have their heart. Anyways, with a heartfelt farewell, I striked out alone. So there you have it, girlie."

"Your story of 'em and their world has struck my heart. Their ways of the land and the nurturing 'em in return echoes peacefully. I see the wrongs of my people and the devastation of it. However, I ain't gonna blame myself. But I will love 'em, care for 'em, and protect 'em," sighed Emily.

The convict took a moment of reflection, before recommencing her narration. "Meanwhile, I can't believe *you*, an orphan and thief, left Ireland for a new start. We are so far away. I admire your determination, but I wish you had a family to go to," said Emily.

"I am glad to hear of an enlightened awareness from you regarding our natives. Progressing forward, may that now forever guide your relationship with them. As to approaching my family, as if I would do that. Why put them through worry? When I was to be a sentence-bound convict like you any time."

"Don't call me that."

"It's the truth, girlie. Tell me your situation, then."

"My father died. We became poor. We went to London to live with my grandmother. Mother and I had to work in 'em factories. Our blunt[1] and Granny's health declined, leaving us even poorer."

Sinking to her knees in weakness, Emily clenched her fist and felt bitter tears filter through her closed eyelids. The Irish girl sank down next to her and laid her arms across Emily's shoulders. Feeling strength from her warm, understanding touch, Emily continued.

"We became banded[2]. I was so banded and miserable, I had to resort to stealing survival necessities with a band of local children. Then, not long before being bonded[3] and passed to Newgate, Granny died. I don't know anything about me mother anymore."

Emily allowed waves of grief to pour from her malfunctioned heart.

"I'm so sorry. It would be utter misery to be in your position. I know the pain that lives inside your soul. I know the pain of telling others your story. I admire you for voicing it to me. It required courage to do so."

"I suppose."

Silence followed but soon lifted.

"Hush those tears. Leave your pain to the Lord. Pain ought to be shared and not dwelled upon."

---

[1] Convicts of the First Fleet used a language called Flash. Blunt, meaning money, is one of the many words that were spoken.
[2] Banded means hungry in Flash language.
[3] Bonded means being taken into custody in Flash language.

"You are right."

Emily opened her eyes, wiping them and taking a deep breath.

"Now I gotta ask, how did you not die yesterday?"

"Oh, once you learn to live with nature and know it to be your protector, your chance of survival increases."

"I see. No, I don't, actually."

"Later youse shall though."

"Emily!" Elizabeth's call rang.

"I gotta go," said Emily.

"You're Emily?"

"Emily Wilson, yes."

"Bloody good name. I'm Caitlin Wells."

"Caitlin Wells. Irish you are and British I am. We are."

The girls shook hands, eyes locked.

"Emily, don't make me search for you," bellowed James. He had returned from marine duties to a worried Elizabeth standing at the door.

"I must go, it must be tucker."

Glancing up, Emily saw the sunset turn the sky to a beautiful array of gold, orange and purple clouds.

"Yes. Be at the same cliff at the 'morrow morning?"

"Yes, of course."

"Now you decide to come back," greeted James as Emily approached. Emily bowed her gaze; her vision fixed on the still brownish grass. James opened his mouth to speak, but Elizabeth numbed his vocal.

"Now dear, leave her with me. You have another long day of duties, and I want to see you well-rested," said Elizabeth, beckoning James to follow her order. Mournfully glancing at the girl and kissing his wife's cheek, James heeded her direction.

"Come eat my dear, I have mutton soup for you, then your cuts must be treated."

"I aint feelin' hunger," protested Emily.

"That's because you're too starved to feel it," said Elizabeth, seating Emily at the table before her tucker.

"You're also recovering from a fever."

Emily stared at the nourishment, sickness and hunger tickling her throat. Her hands tickled in sensation; the memory of her helping Elizabeth gently prepare the tucker arousing her feverish mind. Her nose wrinkled from the smell. Bringing a small meat piece to her teeth, she struggled to chew it before swallowing. Clutching her stomach, Emily vomited miserably.

CHAPTER 4

Late January 1788 had arrived. Emily hurried down the street, glancing every now and then behind her nervously. Her heart leaped for Catlin's presence; her eardrums longing for her round Irish accent. The humid air boiled her skin, her brown dress and petticoat soaked with sweat. The rocks, sticks, bark and dirt bricked her bare feet. Suddenly, a drunk convict man and his mate leapt out at her, tackling her to the ground.

Emily cried "Let me free!"

"Not until you give me a nice long kiss," one slurred.

He drunkenly yanked her to her feet.

"Stop your violation of me," Emily pleaded.

Pulling her in close, the drunk convict swooped in to suck her lips. Emily swiftly stomped on his feet. He dropped her to the ground. The accompanying felon pulled Emily up tightly against his frame.

"Let me go!" Emily struggled.

Roaring with laughter, the drunk convict lazily patted her cheek. He latched his lips onto hers. She squirmed in his arms. Emily hit his cheekbones with all her strength.

"Don't kiss me!" Emily roared.

She moved her head sideways, the man's lips landing on her bosom.

"Girlie girlie, shush now," the slurred voice whispered in her ear threateningly.

Swooping in, his lips again found hers. His strong swoop knocked the two to the hard terrain.

Suddenly, a marine's hands separated them. The drunk convict reached for Emily. The marine thrust him back. Another marine threw Emily over his shoulder. Biting his arm, she heard his enraged cry. She fell, landing with a thud. Scrambling to her feet, she sprinted away, her body aching from the fall.

"Come back!" shouted the marine, desperately chasing her. Emily kept running, shielding herself as she ran through the rough bush terrain. Branches whacked against her arms, and she felt soft leaves brushing against her. Her feet felt the hard soil and rocks. Her cuts gushed blood.

Glancing behind her, she saw the marine struggle to follow her. At last, she reached the cliff.

"Whatever's the matter?" came Caitlin's Irish accent.

There, Caitlin stood, dazed by the cliff.

"I can't explain now, just jump," Emily heaved.

She caught sight of more marines approaching. Entwining their hands, the girls jumped. The marines raised their arms. Water enveloped the girls as their vision adjusted. They surfaced, moving to hug the cliff. Gasping for air, a splatter of bullets greeted their eardrums. Through the haze of the smoke, the girl's spotted the marines with their muskets. Taking a deep breath, they slipped underwater. They swam towards the ocean. At last, they came across sand and sun further down. Dragging themselves to the shore, the girls collapsed, shivering. They rolled over. Head-to-toe to each other, they brought their hands together.

"What happened?" Caitlin inquired.

"Two men, felons like me - one drunk, one not, violated me on my way to the cliff. They kissed me and laughed."

"I hate how men have their way with our bodies. I'm sorry they did that."

"As if I'm aint used to the brats wanting' my body for a child."

"A child?"

"Yes, one tried havin' a child with me on 'em ship."

"And you struggled?"

"No, caught them in the knick of time. Smacked and stomped on 'em feet today."

"Just as you ought to."

Silence followed, soon lifted.

"Caitin, how have you maintained that accent of youse?"

"With a good lad, a young Irish bloke. He too escaped and arrived here in a manner similar to mine. I came across him not long after farewelling the Eora, whose dialect I can speak."

"Eora? Who the bloody hell is that? Is 'em Irish lad still near?"

"You sound like one of those felons already," chuckled Caitlin.

"The Eora are the natives, they took me in until I could walk on my own journey. It was during my journey I came across the Irish lad. He reminded me of my nationality and the accent I almost forgot. He lived alone until he came to my camp," she continued.

"Then where is he now? If he is with you, I ain't gonna believe until meself sees him."

"He is hunting. You will see him if you join us at the campfire."

"I suppose."

A tall and lanky boy with strong Irish features poked at the kangaroo meat strung over the fire.

"I have brought my new friend. This is Emily Wilson," said Caitlin.

"Good to meet youse, I'm Aidan."

The lad shook Emily's hand.

"I have heard of you, Caitlin even told me your story, which appears similar to mine. Let me hear it," she greeted.

Emily gathered her petticoats together and sat on a log. Shivering, the slight wind stung her sodden clothes.

"I suppose so," Aidan swung down beside her.

"I came from Dublin, Ireland, of course. I was orphaned at a young age and lived homeless on the filthy, poor streets. I stole what I needed to survive, and of course I was thrown in the gaols. News came through that the French were going to this great South land. I made my move. I stole the keys off a drunk guard during one of their regular rounds. I escaped and snuck onto a boat to France. I paid thieves with the currency I pickpocketed off locals. The thieves took me to a shipyard. I was smuggled onto the ships. Now here, I am free and in Caitlin's care. It feels awkward though, I being only 14, and her 17."

"Your story saddens me. It's just another of 'em poor and orphaned," Emily hid her tears.

"Now, now. We all lived in similar circumstances, thus we can share the pain and grief," Caitlin reassured.

Sitting beside Emily, she lifted her tear-stained face. Emily smiled and wiped her eyes. The children silently gazed at the bright flames.

Bounding down the terrain and kicking dust into the air, Emily heard the cicadas sing in the brown grass. Lying down and rolling in the grass, she felt the sun prick her flesh. Springing to her feet, she felt a marine wrap their arms around her waist.

"Let me go!" Emily demanded.

"I've got her," the marine said, lifting her.

His strong, muscular arms remained firmly wrapped around her waist.

"What yer doing with me?"

"Taking you to see the flogging of the men who harassed you."

"I don't wanna see."

"Perhaps you might want to see a lady by the name of Elizabeth first?"

"Emily!" cried Elizabeth, kissing her forehead several times.

Emily felt Elizabeth embrace her.

"Why did you run off without telling me? Please don't do it again."

"Yes, Elizabeth," mumbled Emily.

"You're wet and filthy," fussed Elizabeth.

"I'm not," Emily pulled away in protest.

"Come now, thank you sir, I'll take her now."

Taking her hand, Elizabeth hugged her close. She took the girl to the Revelly's cottage.

"I heard what happened," Elizabeth said, helping Emily into a clean, dry dress. It was faded brown with petticoats.

"It doesn't matter," dismissed Emily.

"It does between us."

Elizabeth drew the brush through the girl's hair.

"It doesn't, 'em men own us. James owns you and I. I bet he has his way with women behind your back."

She met Elizabeth's eyes.

"You have been exposed to too many men like the one you encountered. James doesn't harass women, although he treats them like property."

"Then leave him."

"No, dear, I am bound to him through marriage."

"I suppose," Emily yawned, laying her head on Elizabeth's bosom. Her gaze was distant.

"Someone ought to rest," Elizabeth lovingly stroked Emily's hair.

"Elizabeth?"

"Yes?"

"Where do you and James come from?"

"The American colonies. I married my James, born a colonist there, to appease my mother. She wanted his wealth. I only grew to slightly love James. He has spent all of his love on me. He did, however, cheat on me. He had children with other women who loved him. At last, he wanted his own child and forced me to have one. However, a deadly fever took our daughter five years later. He chased more women, violated my body, loosened his grief with drugs, and pursued bad company in his misery. I suffered four miscarriages from his behaviour. My body was even close to getting a disease. At last, we went to war against the British for our freedom and independence. James was one of the first to enlist and take up arms."

"While he liked the ideals of independence and freedom, he supported British ownership of these colonies. Thus, he enlisted with the British. His knowledge of the vegetation, landscape, and environment proved valuable to the British. He met destruction, death, wounds, diseases, illness and more disturbing sights. His letters spoke of the hell he lived in. One that he could never fully describe to me."

"He never spoke of the gunshot wounds I eventually learnt he suffered. After the war, now-sergeant James decided the army was his home. He moved around the colonies. He even rose to the rank of Lieutenant. Eventually, the colonies, now the completely-independent USA, no longer pleased him. In a timely manner, the British marines offered him a commission. He accepted and paid for a passage to London. Years later, James accepted his offer to be a marine on this fleet. Accepting, he took me with him to this strange land. Now here we are."

Emily nodded, the story turning over in her sleepy mind.

"Come now, I can see your exhaustion. Sleep is the medicine right now. While James is still on duty, you will have peace."

CHAPTER 5

Emily woke up to Caitlin whispering in her ear.

"The stars are out. Youse got to see them."

"I can't. James will kill me," greeted Emily.

She thrust her head in his direction to affirm her point.

"Come on now, who gives a flaming hell about him?"

"Fine."

Emily got to her feet and put a finger to her lips to signify silence. She quietly approached Elizabeth. Turning her head sideways, Emily thought for a moment. Bowing her head, Emily planted a kiss on Elizabeth's cheek. The girls ran through the pouring rain, the mud covered their bare feet and splattered their dresses. Nearing marines, the girls ducked low. Cold hands shaded their cigarettes, smoke puffing into the air. Their laughter and masculine voices filled the silence. Broken bottles laid by their feet, their vocals slurring in response. Their observant eyes scanned the surroundings. Glancing behind, Emily saw shapes of more marines travelling down the street.

Vulnerable in their position, the girls moved silently forward. Emily froze, her feet snagging on a branch near them. The voices halted, the figures turning. Collapsing to the ground, Emily moaned.

"Oh, I am raped."

The drunk marines looked to each other in confusion, unsure of what to do. Eventually, they approached the girl cautiously. Their bodies swayed from their intoxication. Their vision blurred. Caitlin meanwhile observed Emily's acting. The marines bent down. Emily leapt to her feet and tackled the nearest marine to the ground. Alarms were raised. Swinging her arm around, she felt her hand collide with a jaw. She heard a thud behind her. Emily felt mud spray her as Caitlin ran in, pushing two into the mud. Springing to her feet, Emily felt a marine knock her down. Having heard the alarms, reinforcements had arrived. They pinned Emily down. Head spinning, and blood filling her mouth, Emily barely saw Caitlin make her escape. Struggling, mud soaking her dress, Emily lost strength. Her last lash fell weak. Lifted into one's arms, Emily flinched at the firm grasp around her waist.

"Let me go!"

"You can get lashed for it, you pretty creature."

"As if that would be."

"I'll see you are."

"Come now, you brat. Lieutenant Revelly will put you in line," another marine ordered.

"No! I don't wanna see him," screamed Emily.

Strength returned to her kicks.

"Shut up."

A muddy hand clamped over her mouth, silencing her.

"You heard her," roared Caitlin.

Running out, she swept the marine off her feet. Shielding her face from the mud, Emily winced in pain. Emily punched the marine unconscious, before wiggling free. Caitlin followed, incapacitating the other marine. Taking Emily's hand, she ran into the bush. Away from the unconscious marines.

Emily had never seen stars until now. London's constantly smoky sky had barricaded her from the beauty. Now she saw the many sparkling white stars dotting the cloudless Australian night sky. The wonder of these beauties caught her breath.

"It's a real beauty, isn't it?" Caitlin pondered.

"We thought you would enjoy the sight," smiled Aidan.

"And I do," Emily said.

"Youse know youse can find youse home amongst them," Caitlin said.

"Like mother and London," said Emily. She turned to Caitlin with a wondrous look.

"Of course. There's always going to be the biggest and brightest star. Youse just got to find it."

Caitlin watched Emily eagerly search for that star.

"I found it!" Emily exclaimed after a moment.

"Yes, that one," Aidan confirmed.

Emily fell silent, mournfully gazing at it.

"There's that brat!" James angrily pulled Emily from the marines.

"I suppose you heard her beat the fuck out of us?" angrily demanded the private.

"By luring us into a fake rape situation," added another.

"Then running off once she was done with us," said the private.

"Not until now," growled James.

"None of that I did!" lied Emily.

Her eyes widened in fear, her body shaking.

"Shut up." roared James.

Clutching her arm, his eyes danced with anger and drilled into hers.

"Don't tell me what to do, I aint yours!" yelled Emily.

Tears streamed down her ghostly pale complexion.

"While you live under this roof, you are mine," roared James.

Emily cried out in pain when his hand hit her cheekbone, leaving her breathless. Clutching her cheek, she felt bruises start to form.

"James, don't hurt her," pleaded Elizabeth, clutching his arm.

"She must be punished. She beat the marines and faked being raped," said James, gritting his teeth.

"She is only young, she knows no better," cried Elizabeth.

"I don't care for your pleas."

James angrily pushed her away. He pulled Emily into an uncomfortable position. Elizabeth cried, holding a hand over her mouth in horror. Continuously thrusting his knee into her stomach, James roared.

"You don't hurt another marine, nor play *poor me*. You are a convict, worthless dirt, a woman whose property is to our better colonists. I will break you, starve you, keep you in the cold or heat, thrash you, or punish you if you do it again. Understand me?"

The pain roared through her, vocal. She felt her wrist break in his grip.

"Understand me?"

"Yes," cried Emily.

Letting go, he grabbed his musket by the door and swung it at her back. Elizabeth hurried to Emily's side. The girl fell to the ground, screaming and writhing in pain. Scooping the screaming girl into her arms, Elizabeth ran through the pouring rain to Surgeon White's hut.

CHAPTER 6

Early February 1788 had arrived. Emily struggled as the marines tied her ankles and wrists to a wooden triangular structure. The convicts in the crowd remained solemn. One of Phillip's men read a scroll describing her latest crime.

"Emily Wilson has been sentenced to ten lashes for injuring marines and faking rape, by Phillip's orders."

The convicts roared with cheers. Some shouted slurs of amusement and assault at the struggling girl. At the nod of Phillip's men, the whip bearers stepped forward.

Emily snarled and picked up the pace of her struggle. The amused whip bearer lifted his whip. Emily would never forget the searing pain as he ripped through her flesh and into sensitive tissue. The shocks of pain and distress buckled her body. She felt the blood gash down her back, absorb her flesh, soak her dress and drip onto the reddish dirt. The convicts went wild, entertained. Meanwhile, the whip bearer brought the ferrule up to announce the second lashing. The ferrule caught some of the damage as it came down on her flesh again. The pain felt worse as it ripped her body and rang in her screams. It felt like a thousand knives were wounding her. James leapt the fence and approached the whip bearer, whispering a few words. The bearer heeded his order, nodding to the marines. They undid the doubled-over Emily. She collapsed to the dirt, feeling the thud of a marine's musket against her stomach on the way. Hot tears of pain stained the dirt.

"Don't tell Phillip of her only two lashings. Make him believe she received the ten," quietly ordered James.

"Yes sir," nodded the whip bearer in understanding.

"What is happening?"

The crowd fell silent. Phillip pushed his way to the front and jumped the fence.

"I was told to stop," chirped the whip bearer.

"Has she had her ten lashes?" inquired Phillip.

Rolling Emily to her side, the marines held her still as Phillip inspected the damage.

"No," confirmed the whip bearer.

"Then finish it," ordered Phillip.

He helped the marines retie Emily to the wooden structure. The screams and pain of every lashing of the whip rang until the last. At last, Emily crumbled weightlessly. Numbed in her pain, she lay sprawled on the dirt. The crowd departed, the convicts discussing the lashings. Elizabeth hurried to Emily's side in tears. But those grieved tears were no match to the pained ones of Emily.

Emily awoke, dazed and numb from the pain. She felt she was in something soft. Feeling the material with her fingers, she gasped. A bed, sheets, and pillow. Her ears heard the faint flapping of the tent entrance, where the sounds of the ocean waves filtered through. Instantly, she knew she was in the tent hospital by the cove[4]. Her vision clearing, she saw the many dirty medical tools laid on the wooden tables.

"Emily, can you hear me?" floated Surgeon White's voice.

"Yes," mumbled Emily, feeling Elizabeth stroke her hair.

"Good. Now, this is going to hurt. I'm going to have to clean those cuts, then apply some oil to them. Hold Elizabeth's hand and stay still on your side," instructed Surgeon White.

She screamed at the first touch on her damaged flesh. The tears soaked her pillow, hands squeezing Elizabeth's. But that was only one of the many he treated and applied oil to. At last, the pain slowly retreated. White slowly sat her up, bringing a glass to her drained lips. The girl thankfully consumed the cool liquid.

"Leave her with me until those cuts have healed some more," Surgeon White instructed Elizabeth.

---

[4] When the fleet had first landed, Surgeon White had established this tent structure himself by the cove. When the general hospital had been established in 1810, White's hospital had been disassembled.

CHAPTER 7

June 1788 has arrived. Emily awoke to shouts of angry convicts and alarmed marines. Without warning, she commenced running to the stores. Marines also hurry down the dusty streets, their muskets at the ready. They answered their calling to cease the chaos. Months after her arrival, just as she'd feared, the colony was struggling and on the brink of starvation. Crimes of theft from the starving, miserable convicts and marines ring through the colony. The supply of fresh nourishment diminished.

In June 1788, the cattle permanently made flight into the bush. The convicts were harshly flogged by whip bearers. Those who supposedly committed the worst of theft in their battle for survival were simply hanged. The summer's heat, the autumn's coolness, and now the biting windy cold; just how the convict's weary and degraded bodies, fights bitterly for urgent adaptation. The unsuitable plants and seeds withers, then perish in the lands they were not born for.

The blistering heat gives way to a freezing winter. Many convicts fall ill with hypothermia and other afflictions. For some, it slays them, in their inadequate clothes. However, the marines only shrug carelessly at convicts who breathe their last breath.

The marines have already had enough of the felons. Even the little crops that grow couldn't be saved from theft. Marines, household-employed convicts and even Emily herself regularly guards their gardens. Even then, they can't always hold back desperate convicts hungrily helping themselves to the gardens.

But there was a percentage of them who didn't escape the traumas of the whips. It was the traumas of her recent fair share of it that keeps the starving Emily clean of theft crimes. Mutton soup, kangaroo stew and emu stew would just keep her alive during the starvation crisis. However, Emily can't escape the scurvy that spreads through the colony as a result of the lack of fresh vegetables. As the convicts suffered forced labour, inadequate clothes for the weather, starvation, flogging, chains, illness, hypothermia and death, Phillip knew he had to act. He sent the Sirius out to the waves to obtain urgently-needed supplies for the colony.

Meanwhile, on shore, the colonists continued their violent interaction with the Aboriginal people. She hears the screams of those slaughtered or wounded at the lamb. She hears the desperate cries, washed by strangling tears, as their souls disappear further inland. She hears stories of convicts who never return from the bush. Colonists steal their dismissing nourishment, and commit atrocities against them, particularly the women.

But the process of colonisation wasn't their deadly enemy. European introduced diseases, to which they had no natural barrier against, depletes their numbers much quicker. Once living humans, their deceased souls litter the water and land. But, those weren't the only victims of dispossession as the conflicts continued. They strike settler's huts, burn their crops, and slaughter their cattle. Ruthlessly, violently, they resist European presence in defence of their traditional land. But in this complex relationship, there was an extent of peace.

There were Aboriginals who showed the colonists how to use the natural resources. They prove to be excellent guides for those defecting further inland. With guidance, Emily develops a humane respect and warmth for these custodians. It comforts her as she witnesses the assertion of European power over stolen land.

But, they can never secede the sovereignty of this colony. A frustrated Phillip would kidnap an Aboriginal man. Employed he is as a tool of communication between the two populations. But they defect to their own clan once relieved from the chains. However, the worst killer of all was the smallpox epidemic in April 1789 at Sydney Cove. While the colonists were to remain free, the Aboriginal peoples would not. 70 percent of their population would be eliminated by this illness.

But these battles weren't the only internal violence during this crisis. Reduction of part rations for everyone and the emptying of stomachs, a number of clashes between convicts and marines occurs. On top of that, tension and desperation were high. And the convicts know that treasure and nourishment, alongside many more valuables, lies in the stores.

Thus, some choose to strike it while marines are coop up in guard duties there. At last, she reached the stores, and her eyes widened at the scene. Convicts vehemently fight to free themselves from the marines. Others were struggling for the muskets.

In horror, she sinks to her knees, as she feels hopeless as a bystander. She runs, covering her ears to the struggles. She ran until she trips over a dying convict. His eyes capture the scars of every horror he has endured, and his situation's fate. That hollowness makes Emily retreat. Suddenly, his bony and withered scarred hand grabs her ankle. Screaming, Emily lashes out at the dying felon.

"Help me!" moans his weak voice.

"How?" Emily simply let the tears flood.

"Get me back to London. Get me far from this hell."

"I can't."

"You-" his body shakes, his face agonisingly twisting. Green, then purple, then nothing fills his complexion. His pinched mouth relaxes to a slight knot. His skin proceeds to coldness, and his glassy eyes gazes upwards.

"No!" she screams, shaking him in vain.

Her tear-filled eyes and tear-stained face turn upwards to the sky. Laying her face on his bony bosom, she shivers from the biting cold.

CHAPTER 8

Laying in the winter sunlight by the cliff, Emily's eyes were caught by the sight of Sirius sailing into Sydney.

"Caitlin, you gotta see this," Emily shook the sleepy girl awake. They glanced at each other, then to the ship.

Turning to Emily, Caitlin demanded "Is that more flaming misfortuned convicts?"

"No, it is our saviour, saving the colony from starvation and collapsing. Many a month we have waited for his sight."

"Oh, I see."

It was May 5th, 1789, and Emily was now 13. In late 1788, the colony moved to more solid structures. Meanwhile, roaring winds blew Sirius West to East. Thus, before she returned to Sydney, she circumnavigated the globe. At Cape of Good Hope, Africa, the Sirius completed the task a desperate Phillip had originally sent her for. A plentiful supply of nourishment and planting seeds.

A fierce storm nearly shipwrecked Sirius, as it sent her around in Tasman's Head. Tasman's Head resided South of Van Diemen's Land, now Tasmania. The sight of Sirius returning to Sydney on that day saved the colony with their supplies. They watched in relieved awe. It even made Emily woop and dance around the rock clearing in joy.

At last, Phillip's desperation to save this new British colony had ridden Emily's fears. No longer would there be internal battles within the colony to fight for its survival, or else to truly perish. But yet, it truly takes the abandoned people to ensure the long-term survival of a colony so far away.

CHAPTER 9

June 1789 had arrived. "Hello. Is this Elizabeth of Lieutenant James Revelly here?" boomed a voice.

Knuckles rapped against a door.

"Who are they?" demanded Emily.

"I don't know, but continue sewing the dress," instructed Elizabeth.

Getting to her feet, Elizabeth curiously greeted the unannounced visitor. Hence, a marine officer, attired in his splendid uniform, stood before the lady. A sword was laid to rest in his sabbath. A polished musket was slung over his shoulder.

Unknown to her, he was Lucas Briggs. Enlisted with the British, he was devoted to their empire, despite American ancestral ties. After active service in the American Independence War, he had arrived in this struggling colony with the First Fleet and his family. Now that their convict servant had taken flight, he was on the search for another. Upon meeting fellow mariner James,

Lucas was astonished by the glorification of Emily's available service.

"Yes, gentlemen. I am the Elizabeth you are looking for. I dare hope you haven't come to report anything unfortunate happening to James."

"No. I wouldn't, for I am not placed in his command."

"Then why are you here, may I inquire?"

"For the services of Emily Wilson, whom you are caring for."

"Seeing you're enquiring after her, let us discuss the matter seated."

Elizabeth swept the visitor to a stool. Gathering her petticoats together, Elizabeth flicked a reassuring smile at the unsettled Emily. Emily watched the lady seat herself beside her. Turning to her sewing, Emily listened to the discussion.

"I need a servant to help my wife care for my children. They are unruly and not the brightest of larks, but they need to know their expected tasks, and demandance to be suitable."

"I know how do 'em sewing, cooking and that lot through Elizabeth's teaching," piped up Emily.

Elizabeth patted her hands with desperation in her eyes. Regret chilled the girl's stomach. Emily's heart skipped a beat, as she realised Elizabeth was battling to save her.

"Do you, now?" Lucas turned to face the alarmed Emily.

"No, she made a mistake. I haven't yet taught her, but soon will," answered Elizabeth.

"That can't be true. James informed me of his wife equipping the felon with womanly and household skills," asserted him smugly.

"Of course James would have eagerly boasted to the marines. I should have known that was the case."

"Yes you should have, my dear. Thus, with this knowledge and after speaking to James personally, I've come to claim her as mine."

"Oh please, can't she complete her tasks during the day, then stay the nights with us?" pleaded Elizabeth.

"No I won't!" Emily screamed in vain.

Dropping her sewing, Emily threw her arms around Elizabeth. Elizabeth allowed her bosom to soak the distressed and distraught tears of the shaking girl.

"Did you not hear me? She is mine now," reiterated Lucas.

"Property, dirt, thief, convict. That's who I am," bitterly pondered Emily.

"I am exiled. I belong to the colony's better colonists, and I ultimately belong to men," she continued.

Silence followed, Emily's gulping tears the only sound. At last, Elizabeth weakly stated.

"I must discuss it alone with the girl in the next room."

Emily allowed Elizabeth to drag her into the second room. Elizabeth tightly hugged Emily, gently resting her chin on the girl's brown wavy hair.

"I don't wanna go!" sobbed Emily.

"Oh my girl, I am afraid I can't keep you any longer. I am afraid your iron-bound chain fate can't be completed in my care. As James vehemently reminds me nightly, you are an exiled convict with a sentence to serve. You are the colony's property, and your sex makes you further belong to men. Now, you are to labour the day as all convicts do.

"You must bear the servant's life bravely. Don't struggle, don't fight. Just hope. Just dream of the door to the better life you may one day forge once you leave your chains for good. Perhaps we may see each other one day. Let unconditional love bind us together, for we may forever be separated in our ways now."

Weak, Emily's head spun as she hit the hard earthen floor. Her body buckled from her knees taking the impact. The strength, the will Elizabeth had forged in her hopeless soul evaporated. It felt like a human hand tore her chest open, crushed her pained heart and carelessly threw it. She felt the words *dirt* and *thief* dampen her soul. She felt the words make her feel worthless in the presence of better colonists. She could only feel Elizabeth's body heave one last time. The body that would collapse, and cry for Emily in many sleepless nights.

"You hate me, don't you?" demanded the Lucas, amused beside Emily in a horse drawn carriage. The bite of the chilly wind numbed Emily's physique in her poor thin petticoats. Marines patrolled the streets in companies. Muskets were slung around their broad shoulders. Cold breath evaporated from bodies wrapped in the warmth of their great coats. The streets were too roamed by free colonists. Cockey and slurred accents rang; signifying the labouring of convicts on the developing dirt roads.

"I do," abruptly confirmed Emily, refusing to meet his eyes.

"Well, perhaps your new tasks awaiting you will be just the medicine."

"As if that would flaming be it."

"Tongue, felon."

"Tongue, sir," Emily smiled at her snap answer, surprising him.

They sat in silence until Lucas announced they had reached their destination. The carriage halted in a timely rhythm.

"Stay here. You felons file out last after your master."

The door swung open and Lucas disembarked. Emily followed at his heel; her hands retrieving her few possessions wrapped in one of Elizabeth's shawls. With a click, Lucas shut the door. Tipping his hat, the driver clicked his tongue. The risen dust from the dirt covered the jogging horse.

"Lucas!" cried a young woman's voice.

Children, youngsters, with one even a toddler, clutched her petticoats.

"Ava, my dear. I have the children's new caretaker and our servant," informed Lucas.

"Good. Bring her in for inspection," ordered Ava, beckoning the children to scatter.

The well-dressed and fed children eagerly heeded their mother's order. Emily followed the marine and his wife. They entered their well-constructed, single-storey stone cottage. She envied the man-made fancy furniture. Their plentiful supply of nourishment left her reeling in anger. Even the dress and well cared-for clothes disgusted her. Of course, marines and non-felons were the better, more important ones in this colony-society.

"Now stand before me," Ava seated herself at the table. She beckoned Emily over. Emily grudgingly stood before her, Lucas towering nearby.

"You're skinny as a rail, and pale as a ghost."

Emily flinched at the bony fingers feeling her physique.

"You better eat my tucker, it will fatten you up and give you the strength you require," said Ava.

"Yes, I thought so too," Lucas murmured. Silence followed, then was interrupted with Lucas desperately stating, "My dear, I'm sure she is the right fit."

"She'll do for now," Ava nodded to Lucas. She turned to Emily.

"Now, the responsibility of the children is in your hands. The housework is too. You will be flogged for any disobedience. You are to obey every given command or direction. You are to sleep in the kitchen, to ensure sustained warmth and deterrent of thieves. You are to enforce discipline and manners in the children. Any failures in that, as well as lack of compliance in your sleeping arrangements will result in flogging. Understood?"

Emily nodded.

"Good. You may meet the children now," Ava's songlike call brought a scurry of feet to her side.

"Remember their names," said Lucas.

"This is Thomas,"

The lanky and slender lad of 10yrs stepped forward. His sideways-clipped brown hair, blue eyes, narrowly-shaped nose and discerning mouth fit him well. Emily bit her tongue as he bumped hips with her. Winking, Thomas didn't flinch as Lucas flashed a stern frown in his direction.

"This is William."

Strongly resembling his father's appearance, the 11-year-old lad slightly bowed his head in her direction.

"This is Martha."

Sharing a blended resemblance to both her parents, the 9-year-old smiled slightly.

"This is Mary."

The toddler strongly resembled her mother's delicate features. Screeching in joy, Mary was held back by Martha.

"This is Emily, your new caretaker," Lucas introduced the unentertained convict girl to the children.

The children whined in unison.

"Silence. I have made my decision."

Lucas watched the whining faces cringe. Unable to bear her emotions, Emily ran outside and threw herself at the dead yellow grass. Kicked, screamed, and cried in misery she did.

CHAPTER 10

October 1789 had arrived. "Be good to her my children," was what Emily last remembered as she witnessed the mother kiss each youthful face before sleep bestowed them.

But of course, the boys wouldn't do that to such worthless dirt as her. Torment her, they did. Kicking her, punching her, catcalling her, vehemently name-calling her and just about every other tormentor's attack they could bestow upon the torn girl. The thought of another thrashing by the whip or Lucas' hands kept her from complaining. It internally killed her every time, but what side would she gain, being a felon? She was just dirt, a woman, property, and that was that. No questions asked, it confirmed Emily's position in the colonial society.

Ava and Lucas were no better as the days bore by. Approaching fourteen, Emily's sexuality had further developed. Her appearance moulded into that of a beautiful young lady. But this growth couldn't be saved from her master's brutality. Lucas was the one to severely punish her for every wrongness. Emily's complaints and protests of the labour, as well as sexual exploitation of her, brought fierce crashing upon her bones.

Thus, Emily spent many sleepless nights, either wishing herself deceased, or in Elizabeth's unconditional love. Other times, she thought about taking flight to her Irish friends in the bush. But deep inside, she knew that better days would one day arrive.

The boys were the worst of her misery. Their continuous torments and mocking laughter made her want to rebel. But their position in the hierarchy and the power of this household refrained Emily from it. But frustration ripened, her outrage at such vile treatment eventually shone.

And it did one day, while cleaning the table after mutton soup.

"Convict girl, I heard you sobbing like a baby last night. Was it for that stupid lady?" William tormented.

"So what, brat? Me had enough of yer whining' voice," Emily snarled.

"You sound like a whining baby," mimicked Thomas with a giggle.

"I couldn't agree more," chirped the boys in unison.

They shakily rose to their feet.

"You livered beast," angrily roared Emily.

Grabbing the wooden spoon, she bent William over the table. Just the satisfaction she gained, months of her agonised anger and grief, lashed the screaming boy. Just the pleasure from the screams that rung from every *thwack* upon his backside. Just how she wished the other children would stop raising alarms through desperate and distraught strangled cries. At last, Ava came hurrying to her flock.

"You beast!"

Grabbing her arm, Ava yanked Emily apart. The mother inspected the reddened backside.

"They were humiliating me!" cried Emily, tears stinging her enraged eyes.

"And what does it matter?" Ava demanded. "You hurt my angels, you dirty shit."

"Stop callin' me that," growled Emily.

She jerked to the side. Ava's hand brushed past the girl's physique.

"I ain't yer property to be laboured and exploited," Emily said.

"Silence that evil talk. No man would bear to hear it."

"Then I can't bear this hell anymore. If the Lord would let me, I would let death relieve me."

"I demand an end to your beastly thoughts."

"If only yer get rid of me."

"Through what?"

"Surrendering' me to Elizabeth."

"As if you belong to her realm," roared Ava.

A mocking laughter rippled her throat.

"You don't own me. Elizabeth deserves my ownership."

"She doesn't. You're mine now."

Ava threw Emily onto the hard earthen terrain and held her down. As she went to wack her backside, lines on her back's flesh caught Ava's eyes.

"Don't touch them," Emily struggled in her hold.

Petticoats were thrown back, the permanent scars of her flogging revealed.

"So you have been flogged. Well then, perhaps a beating from Lucas is the medicine to cure your evil ways. I shall fetch him. Thus, you shall wait in this very seat for him."

Ava threw Emily upon the stool, departing in a hurry. Just the hurt, the anger that killed her fast-beating heart. At last, she couldn't bear it, and made her dash down the streets of Sydney. Ran, she did. The dirt, rocky paths barely denting her toughened feet. But her physique proved little in strength. She buckled to the path in an alley. Heaving for breath, Emily froze.

CHAPTER 11

"Look at that young pretty creature," whispered a shadow.

"How are we going to sneak her back with us to the men's tents? She'll scream in the sack."

"Then we gotta knock her out."

Emily saw the shadow of two older men, well-known thieves, approach her in their ragged, ill-fitted, loose, and stripy clothes. She tried to move, but without strength, could not prevail. Instead, a dirty hand clamped her mouth tightly shut. The rising scream died in her dry throat.

"Hello pretty lady, I know some men who would enjoy your attraction."

Those were the last words she remembered, before cold hands knocked her unconscious. Then, those hands dropped her in the sack.

Faces swarmed her blurred vision. Voices banged her aching head. She felt weak, laying on the hard earthen floor of the humid tent. A hand reassuringly patted hers.

"Come now, girlie."

Emily rose from the ground with the voice, shakily buckling into strong, muscular arms. But the rustling of her petticoats sharpened her daze and confusion. She screamed, struggling to return. Mocking laughter killed her eardrums.

"Let go!" Emily pulled against his strength. The hands grabbed her waist and pulled back.

"Lay her down."

Emily struggled, lanky arms swinging her onto the blankets. The men hungrily hovered nearby. A lanky and handsome one threw himself on top. His lips latched onto hers, his hands gripping her bosom. Struggle, she did, against his weight, until they fell with a thud. She leaped, her physique wincing in pain. She felt the wind knocked out of her lungs. She felt arms hold her close.

They spiralled sideways to the clay. Rolling inwards, Emily violently lashed out, until he let go with cries of pain. She attempted leaping for the still tent entrance, but hands yanked her downwards.

"Come now girlie, there's no use rebelling."

"Hand me to 'em marines!"

"Not yet. You can sleep the night with us."

Agreement rose in the air. Hands strangled the girl's limbs and forcefully fed her into the sack. She kicked and cried, the sack heaved into position. Worn rope tied the victim around the wooden beam supporting the tent roof. Emily heard the amused whispers of the convict men leaving to their assigned labour. Men, who left her to dangle from the supporting beam.

The fall of footsteps before her alarmed Emily. She cried with pain, the sack thumping onto the earth. She reeled from the light endowsing the sack. She felt hands guide her out. A tall, handsomely featured, and masculine marine gazed back. His hand loosely held hers. His dark green eyes tenderly gazed into hers with a curiosity. His black hair was crusted by thin dust and brushed back from his forehead. His marine's uniform complemented his white complexion. "Thank you, whoever you are."

"Jackson."

"Jackson. You can let go," Emily batted his hand away.

"I have heard about you."

"You have?"

"Yes, stories I know concerning you, Emily Wilson. They come from the Revelly's and your current owners."

"And I don't wanna discuss 'em," Her eyes lowered from his intent gaze.

"One day you will, pretty girl."

"Have you found her?" called a deep voice.

"Yes, I'm taking her home myself though."

"I can walk alone, thank you," protested Emily. She stepped forward.

"A lady never walks alone," Jackson wrapped a firm arm around her waist.

"I'm a felon. I ain't any lady," asserted Emily with a flinch.

"Your difference doesn't matter to me in this situation," Jackson loosened his grip.

"I suppose," muttered Emily.

CHAPTER 12

Emily sat on the steps of her master's cottage; her vision gazing out to the boys playing with other youngsters on the dusty streets. Dirt stained their tanning complexion as they tackled one another. Her tired arms cradled the sleeping toddler. Her knees provided protection.

How free these youngsters were; the road gangs rattling past them. Freedom she had once lavished, but no more it breathed. Now it was lost in the breeze of the past. And it pained her heart to see this liberty in these unknowing children. Youth, who saw the scrub and dirt of a convict. But a minority who yearned to comprehend these felons against their parent's hatred of them.

And Emily had come to the conclusion that Martha was one of them. For torment she didn't. Catcall she didn't. Strike her she didn't. For Martha yearned to understand her past. Her heart longed to connect with a girl whose past she could never understand. But, Emily knew she could gain awareness. Thus, with gentle coaxing, the wounded Emily opened her woes, suffering, and losses. A gentle, compassionate hand was lent to the tumour and tears.

And that humanity had rekindled fledging hope in Emily. It gave her strength to see past her abuse and to a future calling for her. She felt reconnected to the wisdom of Elizabeth's parting words. For Martha came to her cries at night. She came to her hunger with sacrifices of her meals. She preached hope and comfort into a worn soul. Thus regenerated and wiser had Emily become in this light.

And Emily was deep in these thoughts when Martha seated herself beside Emily. Sensing her exhaustion, Martha gathered the sleeping toddler into her sisterly arms. Emily stretched out her legs.

"My dear, you appear exhausted. If only I could settle you in bed, but mother would punish you for neglecting your duties."

"I thank thee, but it aint to be Martha," smiled Emily.

"Well, I hope you can be free like us one day."

Emily meets the childish eyes; curiosity and hope flicking in her gaze. Then she sharply turned away, knowing how little this child understood of a convict's fate. "I may or may not be. I am a convict, we ain't all gonna be free."

"But Emily dear, have faith in the Lord. I feel your time of remediation before our rulers will come with only the right moment," Martha clasped Emily's limp hand.

"I suppose."

"Emily!" roared Lucas, "Where is my tucker?"

"I gotta go," sighed Emily. Scurrying to her feet, Emily heeded Luca's order.

CHAPTER 13

December 10th, 1789.

Emily boiled in the humid air and dread of her fate. She stood on a cart beside an auctioneer. She silently gazed at the crowd of convicts and marines. Grieved of her conduct, Ava and Lucas made the decision to sell her.

"Come now, surely one of you would want her? She's skinny and tall. But she can do all the servant's work, bear children, and rear 'em youngsters," the auctioneer boosted.

"I bet she can!" Emily flinched at a nearby convict as his hand eagerly ruffled her petticoats. With a deathly glare, she shakily snatched her petticoats back.

"Come now gentleman, restrain yourselves! Any bids surely?"

"Two shillings!" called one.

"Oh gentleman, you're being too generous. Come now, don't be afraid to bid higher."

"As if we wouldn't!" joked one.

The crowd roared in agreement. Again, Emily snatched her petticoats back from a nearby sheepish man.

"Come now gentlemen, make your bets!" encouraged the auctioneer.

"Three and a half shillings!"

"Four shillings!"

"Three shillings!"

"Surely higher?" stirred the auctioneer. She clutched his arm in weakness, the auctioneer resting his hand on hers. She couldn't bear the crowd fighting, yelling, and bidding excitedly over each other for her.

"Three shillings can't be it," called a voice.

"Excellent, young man!" praised the auctioneer.

"Then ten pounds should do."

"Perhapes, perhapes," flirted the auctioneer with a wink.

"No, eleven pounds should!"

"Not if someone offers a higher bid," asserted the auctioneer.

"Let me see her closely." She struggled as she was lifted down for inspection. "She's too skinny!" Emily scrambled back onto the cart.

"Then, you must fatten her up to satisfy yourself."

"Of course! I will gain satisfaction from fattening her up. Overall, the most important ideals is that she can do all the servant work and birth wonderful youngsters."

"You are very right, gentleman," agreed the auctioneer. A slight bow of his head showed this agreement.

"I bet 10 and a half then!"

"10 and a half pounds or shillings? Well, you are catching my heart. Any higher bids?"

"Twenty pounds!" boomed Jackson's voice. Falling silent, the crowd parted. Jackson presented himself before the auctioneer and Emily.

The now 13-year-old Emily blankly gazed at the marine. Glancing away; she refused to meet the love-sickened eyes of a marine she didn't love. Her eyes happened to catch the site of the marines inspecting a line of women in the distance. She saw some of the women removed to the nearby dark blue coats. Of course, the removed women were the plummist and prettiest who were these marine's first picks.

She knew those selected women would become the wives of these marines. She knew the remaining women would meet the same fate as her, auctioned off to the highest bid. Then of course, they would become the property of that buyer for as long as they were wanted. Just like now.

"This wrench has been sold to this young man for twenty pounds!" announced the auctioneer. Pointing to the amused Jackson, the auctioneer's news brought roaring cheers.

Jackson passed his pounds to the auctioneer then lifted the unfazed girl to the ground. She simply allowed him to support her weakened legs to a nearby stump. The roars of more women being sold angered Emily. She knew that each silent, weak, woman on the cart would be worn by labour and sexual exploitation.

Emily knew that would last until their sentences expired. Sentences that would be closed to freedom. She knew the vulnerability of standing upon the cart beside the voice of the auctioneer. She understood the fear and dread of the unknown. She knew what it felt like to be examined and touched. She knew the greater vulnerability and danger being a woman brought.

She knew what it meant to be property before and after standing on that very cart. Thus, each sale brought tears of pain, grief, understanding, and anger to Emily's vision. She wanted to leave the crowd and their bids. She wanted to drown herself in the cool ocean. Yet, she desperately wanted to see Elizabeth and her mates. But Jackson drew amusement from every auction. All she could do was lay her head on his board shoulder. There, she could close her vision to darkness.

CHAPTER 14

February 1790 had arrived. Emily grew to hold no knowledge of the outside world. Confined, she was within the stone wall's of Jackson's cottage. The only knowledge she grew to hold was the routine of her occupation. Every morning, she arose from the hard-earthen terrain floor to prepare Jackson's nourishment. As he ate, she stood by his side to see him satisfied. Then she assisted his well-fed physique into his marine's coat.

Her back broke from the dusting that tickled her nose and dried her throat. Her hands sustained burns and cuts from taking care of his nourishment. Her arms aced from the swing of the heavy axe splitting the firewood. The heat sweated her back, the sweat clinging to her dress and back flesh. Her arms and back aced from the grind of house labour. Exhaustion struggled to nightly tether the kitchen fire.

The only strength she gained to endure the toil was from the scraps of tucker Jackson left her. Of course, he only cared for her sexuality in the quietness of night. But his unfazed gaze turned into that of burning love.

Punishments became less, her sleeping arrangements changed, her lips bore more forceful kisses, and more tucker was forced into her shrunken stomach.

The tumour, the wounds, the confusion, bode Emily down. The only chance she had to indulge in her thoughts were the daily collection of their rations from the stores. But despite his firm grasp of her, Emily was able to enjoy the mateships of her Irish friends. Many a night they breathed together singing, dancing, acting, and star-gazing around the bright campfire. Yet, the kindle doesn't always burn brightly when secrets are discovered.

CHAPTER 15

March 1790 had arrived. Emily abruptly woke to the sounds of heavy boots bashing their way through the thick bush. The flash of red coats, the sun catching their gold buttons, and the reflective shininess of their muskets caught her eyes. The bicen hats hopped along.

Shaking Caitlin, Emily screamed and wailed. Tears streamed down her drained face. Her voice screamed, "The marines are coming!"

The desperation to save her Irish mates from the oncoming slaughter hammered her soul. It made her shake, cry, scream, and wail to the sleeping children. She knew every approaching step brought no mercy. She knew she had to stir her mates to consciousness.

"Stop shaking me,"murmured Caitlin. Sitting upright, Caitlin sprung to the alarm. She could hear the approaching marines. Her violent shakings and alarms brought Adian aboard.

With the party encircling them, they faced no escape. If they were to charge, the bayonet would thrust them to death. So they clutched each other close, praying with closed eyes to the Lord. Every weakly murmured word strengthened their souls against the approaching force. Their warmth and mateships felt like the mightiest of shields. However, the reality of marines tearing them apart broke their forged shield.

"Don't kill them!" pleaded Emily. Desperately she struggled, as the marines held her hands hostage behind her back.

"How dare you escape my clutch!" Jackson roared. His hand knocked the breath from her lungs.

"You don't own me!" Emily heaved. Tears blurred her vision and her lungs laboured for breath. She fell to her knees. The marine fell with her to maintain his grip.

"I do," Jackson knelt before her. He deathly met her eyes. "I never gave you permission to be with them. I didn't even hold knowledge of your nightly gatherings with these children." Going pale as a ghost, Emily felt weak. She fell back in her captivator's arms. "I heard you dismiss the fire, so I was aroused. Of course, you were leaving without my permission. Thus I silently followed you till you reached this site."

"How could you?" weakly demanded Emily. Sparks of anger brightened her shocked eyes. Thrusting herself forward, she roared, "How could you, you livid beast?!"

"Because I had a right to know, you devil!" Jackson raged. His lips curled into a smirk for he was amused by her anger and struggles. "I know their connections with the blacks," continued Jackson smugly. "I had the pleasure of hearing these children share their stories and thoughts of these blacks with you. My gaining of this knowledge is thanks to my spying. Thus it is time for your relationship with them to end.

Emily screamed; the marines pinned Caitlin down. Adian launched himself forward. A loud bang sounded and smoke filtered into the air. He crumbled and squirmed. Blood poured. A shaking hand covered his gaping wound to his throat.

"No!" roared Emily, breaking free. Running forward, she saw the shock and desperation fill his eyes. Horror numbed her. The marines observed the dying child and a horrified Emily.

How helpless Emily felt seeing the blood drain his soul. The loss of breath suffocated him to death. At last, the desperately squirming and writhing Adian went lifeless. His frozen eyes rolled to Emily's crying ones. His bloodied hand banged like a weightless leaf against the terrain.

Her outrage and despair roared from her vocal. The tears struck the deceased child. She wailed, rocked herself, and kissed his cold cheeks several times. Hands yanked her back. She was forced to face Caitlin. She let the marine keep her head still and bend her arm towards him. She let another clamp her mouth shut.

Her eyes widened. She desperately thrust herself about. Her rebellion was checked with marines grabbing her struggling limbs. Caitlin clutched her naked physique.

Closing her eyes, Emily muffled in retort at a slap forcing them open.

Screams pricered the air. Emily violently squirmed at the sight of Jackson raping Caitlin. Caitlin wailed. Her hands numbly clutched the laughing Jackson. Emily felt weak, her body going numb. Jackson's smirk washed her with anger. Biting the hand, Emily struggled loose.

Springing to her feet, Emily felt her head thud onto the terrain. Weight crushed her down and lips latched onto hers, as demanded by Jackson. Squirming, Emily struggled to breath. A loud bang deafened Emily's eardrums. At last, Caitlin felt her tormented soul relieved to Heaven.

Jackson threw a sack over her head. She thrust it off and took a big gulping breath. The marine pushed himself to his feet. Again, the sack was thrown over her head and Emily's vision met darkness. She felt the strong arms of Jackson drag her to the hospital.

"What did the brats teach you?" demanded Jackson. Surgeon White silently stood nearby.

"Nothing," sobbed Emily, "Leave me alone!"

"Not until you answer me!" Jackson doubled Emily over.

"Their language! Their lifestyle! Their ceremonies! Their games!" screamed Emily. Her shaking body was seared by pain.

"I knew it!" trumphainted Jackson with a roar. Turning to Surgeon White, he demanded "Inspect her for any signs of sexual exploitation and diseases. I want to make sure her sexuality carries no transmittable diseases. I will deal with her brainwashing alone later. I have someone to announce too."

Elizabeth Revelly had become severely weakened by many sleepless nights. Sleepless nights that she spent sobbing for Emily. James became worried by her depression and clumsiness. He had called upon the surgeon many times. Despite his efforts, and that of his Indigenous helper, Elizabeth wouldn't budge.

Thus a convict woman was temporarily loaned for house labour. Elizabeth spent her days by the window. Her vision was tormented by ghostlike memories and images of Emily. But that figure of Jackson approaching the cottage with a sense of urgency caught her off guard. Inviting himself in, Elizabeth greeted the stranger.

Blinded by anger, Jackson roared out Emily's secrets. Shocked, Elizabeth fell to her knees and clutched her heart.

"You knew about it! Emily told me she spent her nights with them from the moment she met the girl here."

"I didn't!" Elizabeth firmly asserted. She burst into renewed tears.

"I am warning you. You may not have been aware of her activities, but you know of it now. Now you also know of my temper. If she escapes to this refuge you must immediately call me. Here I will rape her myself before your eyes."

Elizabeth mumbled in understanding. Once he had gone, her body shutdown and fainted.

Emily laid awake beside Jackson. She glanced into the night darkness. Her mind still fought to register the slaughter. The nightmares and emotional torment of it made her want to scream. It even made her want to brutally slaughter Jackson in revenge. But she knew better than to do either. Yet, she knew she couldn't bear Jackson's emotional rages, sexual exploitation of her, and labour exploitation of her anymore. Even the wise words Elizabeth parted with no longer mattered in her torn soul.

Quietly, she slipped out of bed. Quietly she tiptoed to Jackson's moonlit musket. Freeing the bayonet, Emily saw the moonlight catch the glint of the blade. Shakely she turned it over in her hands. Suddenly the slaughter flashed before her vision. Her vision became blinded by struggles, gunshots, deaths, frozen faces, raping, and kissing. Screams deafened her eardrums.

She collapsed to her knees and bandged her head to dizzyness. She fought not to scream and cry, even though she desperately wanted to. Pain seared her soul. Standing to her feet, Emily violently swayed side to side. Her hands gashed dark blood, the fingers tightly curled around the blade. Desperately she went to thrust the blade into her fast beating heart.

Hands collided and the blade clattered to the ground. Shaking hands pinned her to the ground. Emily vehemently screamed, cried, and kicked at Jackson. Alarms were raised. She was removed to Surgeon White's care. Little did she know, Jackson finalised his long awaited wish.

CHAPTER 16

Late 1790.

Emily's worst dread had arrived. Now, she solemnly waited for three marine wives to accompany the bride girl.

Jackson had gained permission from Phillip to marry the convict girl. Fearing the escape of his bride, Jackson kept her prisoner. For three weeks, Emily felt the chains burden her waist and ankles. She became even paler, distraught, and refused to eat tucker. It only angered the groom, who took to force feeding in many struggles.

Now, Emily sat dutifully by the door. The arrival of her bridal party stirred her to reality.

Emily hated her marriage. The minister's welcoming words made her feel like an outcast in an unconsented marriage. The vows exchanged meant nothing to her bitter heart. She refused to kiss, but instead felt Jackson's lips feel hers. The slipping of the ring on her slightly thinner finger made her flinch.

Her wedding dress not only resembled her position in the colonial society, but also her inferiority to others. The stains, the rips, the fade; her brown petticoats were her only article of clothing. Roses and daisies adorned her hair. Her bricked feet wiggled in the flat black slippers Jackson proudly purchased for her.

But that was the least of her worries. She shrank back into a thin-railed physique. Her back again broke from the toil of the house labour. However, Emily narrowly escaped death for a second time.

CHAPTER 17

Middle 1791 had arrived. Moaning, Emily cried out in pain. Clutching Surgeon White's hand, she cried and screamed in the tent hospital bed.

How the pain seared her shaking body to exhaustion. Exhaustion that struggled to birth the child from her thin-railed physique. The encouraging grasp of his hand provided no reassurance. Not even the hands of the convict woman acting as a midwife reassured Emily.

"Come now, Emily. One more push is all you need," encouraged Surgeon White.

The pain killed her vocal cords. Closing her eyes, Emily shivered as the hands pulled the screaming baby from her body. She felt the surgeon's hand slip from hers. She heard the footfalls of the surgeon departing to fetch Jackson. She felt the convict sit by her side. She heard the wails of the baby being held close to the convict's bosom. She felt the blankets be brought to her chin.

How Emily had fought against Jackson as he undressed her. How she screamed and wailed as he forcefully bowed her to sex. How she withered at the internal workings his sexuality brought her. How the unconsented sex flashed memories of his raping and slaughter of Caitlin.

Surgeon White had warned him of the severe illness it would bring upon the girl. And as warned, Emily had become severely ill. It left her withering and weakened to a life threatening state. She couldn't talk, her limbs felt numb. Her complexion turned a deadly shade. She wanted more than ever to be relieved to the internals of death, Heaven. She would have closed her blurred vision, if it weren't for the voices of Jackson and the surgeon stirring her.

"Jackson, I warned you and you didn't listen. She must stay with me until I feel fit that she is strong enough," asserted Surgeon White.

"I can't care for the child as a full-time marine," protested Jackson.

"You heard me! She is not leaving my care until she is well again. You nearly killed her with this child, so spare her the dignity. If she takes months, then so be it!" hissed Surgeon White.

"Fine," Jackson gathered the newborn into his arms. The convict vacated the seat for the marine.

Emily opened her eyes to Jackson sitting beside her. He knew her eyes wanted to wound his emotions like he did to her. But he knew the illness had depleted her strength. The newborn strongly resembled the man she vehemently despised. Only the mother's inherited eyes could bring a weak smile to her lips.

"I shall name our son Henry," Jackson tenderly tickled the wiggling newborn. Passing the convict woman Henry, he leaned in to kiss her unmoving lips.

Yanking him back, Surgeon White affirmed, "That's enough now."

"What with the tears now?"implored the Surgeon White. Appearing by her side with a lit candle, Emily indulged in her tumour.

"I want Elizabeth!" wailed Emily.

"Elizabeth Revelly?"

"Yes."

"Please, calm your sorrow. I will fetch her now."

"My darling Emily, silence those tears now. Release your sorrows to me."

The voice of the worried and shaken Elizabeth stirred Emily. The entwining of their hands made the girl cry harder. Through much whispered and strangled words, Emily informed Elizabeth of everything that happened since departing her care. She made sure to include the forced sex.

At last, Emily pleaded, "Please take me! Convenience James to buy me off Jackson. Jackson is gonna break me to death. He's already exploited me body and used me for house labour. I can better tolerate James' hatred and punishments of me than Jackson. If you don't take me, I will commit suicide."

"Emily, don't you dare commit suicide!" roared Elizabeth in desperation. She clutched the girl's hand and held it to her bosom.

"What am I to do?" demanded Emily in despair. "Bear that monster and his treatment of me until I die?"

"No, just stop thinking about that. Listen to my voice. Let me discuss the matter with James. Just please, I can't bear for you to commit suicide. My heart is broken enough."`

"I suppose."

CHAPTER 18

"Jackson, you know I outrank you enough to claim Emily. You know better than to keep her to serve your selfish interests. You know your grasp on her has ended. You know you must hand back that ownership of her to me. I owned her first," urged James, sitting across from Jackson.

James' eyes drilled into Jackson. Nearby was a healthy older convict girl attending to Henry. Elizabeth clutched James' arm. Her heart raced.

"I will not give her back. I may have brought another felon, but Emily is my wife now," gritted Jackson.

"No, you will divorce her and return us Emily's ownership," asserted James.

"I refuse to do that! I married that pretty creature out of burning love," refused Jackson.

"Love? You forced her to marry you. You forced her to have sex with her. Now you have bestowed a severe illness upon her. It has even nearly killed her. How is that a marriage out of love?"

"I don't care whether you call that love! She is my dirt, property, wife!" roared Jackson.

James shrugged Elizabeth off. Enraged, he launched himself at Jackson. The two men collided, diving on top of each other to the terrain. Elizabeth guided the convict girl and Henry to safety. Then she picked up her skirts and raced for help. Jackson stretched forward to grasp the lady.

Gripping Jackson, James launched him at the wooden shelf. Wood, utensils, and pots bruised Jackson. A cloud of dust ticked his throat and nose. Enraged, Jackson sweeped his opponent to the ground. James swung his arm around, hocking Jackon's neck in. Jackson vehemently withered and roared in blinded anger. Breaking free, his punch sent James reeling backwards. Thrusting his knee into James, Jackson knocked him unconscious.

Emily screamed. Jackson yanked her off and held her close to his frame. Wrapping an arm around her waist, he pushed a shotgun into her hair. Elizabeth and Surgeon White came wheeling around the corner.

"It's over. Emily is mine forever," smiled Jackson.

"Put the gun down Jackson. Don't you dare shoot her!" Cautiously, Surgeon White approached him.

"Back off!" roared Jackson. He pushed the shotgun in further. Emily wailed. She reached for a horror shrunken and pale Elizabeth. The girl's complexion turned a deathly shade.

"Let go of her now!" Surgeon White yelled.

Emily meets Jackson's eyes. Flames of anger danced in his eyes. It felt like it burnt hers. Thrusting Emily to the ground, Jackson lowered the shotgun to her head. Suddenly, hands flashed. The shotgun clattered to the ground. Jackson sprawled onto the floorboards. Marines encircled him. James towered over his collapsed body. Elizabeth hurried forward. Emily numbly clutched her arms. She buried her head in the darkness of her bosom. Elizabeth laid her chin on the girl's hair. They held each other close.

"It's okay darling, you are safe now," reassured Elizabeth.

CHAPTER 19

August 1791 had arrived. Emily felt cool in the shade of Elizabeth's shawl. Excitement sounded from the crowd of convicts. Her eardrums reeled from the vibration. The worried eyes of the lady regularly glanced at the girl's uneasiness.

Jackson limply allowed the marines to tie the worn ropes around his neck. His ears fell dead to the reading of his crimes by one of Phillip's officer's.

"Jackson has been proved of raping servual women, and abusing and exploiting his divorcee. He has been proven guilty of stealing from convict rations," projected the officer.

The convicts roared in agreement and threw rotten tucker at the silently fusing marine. The girl buried her face deeper in Elizabeth's bosom. The pain of his crimes, and the cheating of her, broke her already shattered heart. Elizabeth sensed it and laid her head on hers as a ressurance. The girl let her heart feel this warmth. Warmth, that vibratcd in their entwined hands.

"On the order of Captain Aruthur Phillip, Jackson has been sentenced to death!" Another deafening roar of cheers greeted this announcement.

Emily lifted her tear stained gaze to the livid marine. A party of fellow marines removed the platform from underneath. Suspended, Emily shakily covered her mouth at the squirming figure suffocating. Yet, it brought her happiness. It relieved her to think that she no longer had that monster. It brought her a sense of justice to see the suffocating, feared eye, gasping, and purple faced marine. That sense of justice brought her pleasure.

At last, Jackson went numb and his eyes rolled back. A deafening roar of cheers accompanied his spirit to the internals of Hell. Emily burst into renewed tears of happiness and victory. The Revlley's had won the fight for Emily Wilson. She was divorced, approved by Phillip. Phillip, who gave the Revelly's permanent ownership of the girl. After months of separation, exploitation, emotional turmoil, and tumour, Emily has been reunited with the woman who truly loved her. Thus no more tears were needed. There was to be only happiness in her physical, mental, and emotional recovery. A recovery that would take place in the tent hospital. There, she would rebuild her strength. Surgeon White would closely watch over her. Then afterwards, he would watch the tearful reunion between Emily and the Revelly's on a beautiful, sunny, windless, and hot day.

CHAPTER 20

September 1791 had arrived. At last, the Lord had bestowed upon the girl freedom and warmth! Emily never completely recovered from the trauma. Nor did she ever forget the hell she had endured. The emotional toil of it resulted in the first five months being full of nightmares. Nightmares that ridden Emily to screaming and wailing. Only the reassuring warmth of Elizabeth or the surgeon could bestow peace upon her mind.

Fear refrained her from being near men who weren't the kind faces of James or Surgeon White. She curled into a protective ball and refused to leave her cocoon. It suited Surgeon White well. For, he kept Emily under his tent hospital care for the five months it took to recover her health from the severe illness. The first step into the sandy banks of the cove on a beautiful spring day rattled her. The throng of convicts, free colonists, marines, and officers, especially men, alarmed Emily.

Elizabeth coaxed Emily to eat tucker until she gained a slightly thinner physique. Emily revolted at such an introduction of nourishment. However, she grew to trust the coaxing. Elizabeth knew that the Lord's bestowment had to be executed. Thus James and her let the girl rejoice in childhood frolic. Slowly, gently; Elizabeth guided the fear-ridden girl into the new and better world awaiting her. Slowly, Emily found that inner courage and strength to face this world.

Emily was introduced as an adopted child of the Revelly's to the marines and their wives. They then passed the introduction onto their children. Earning their mateships, Emily ran rampage on the dusty dirt streets and the yards of their homes. And these children felt the scars of Emily's old childhood. An old childhood, now something of the past. Instead, Emily is now forging a new and better life. This was embraced and helped to be nurtured by her new mates. However, she could never forget the slaughter of her Irish friends. She could even feel the motherly and grandmotherly smiles upon her from the internals of Heaven.

Emily found wonder in the reading, dancing, writing, singing, and piano Elizabeth taught her. At first she struggled with frustration to comprehend her new skills. Every frustration drew Emily determination to persist with. Many nights she spent gritting her teeth. At last, she had won and impressed the Revelly's with her new knowledge.

James had changed. His internal sadness had ripened into his true colours. His soul, heart, brimmed with a kind, respectful, and gentle fatherly nature. He took Emily on many walks around the cove and visits to Surgeon White.

He taught her how to be an excellent horse rider with the colony's calvary stallions. He played many games with her. She quickly grew to deeply love his warmth and change of character.

Sundays were one of her favourites. The Revelly's took it upon themselves to nurture the girl's religious beliefs at the Christian services. Thus she became open to the Lord. She felt his guidance steer her. She felt his love and warmth shield her. The warmth and love of the Revelly's felt just the same way. The words, sermons and readings wonderly captivated her. It brought her internal strength and meaning.

A sense of belonging came in the playing with her mates and the fussing of mothers. Again, she drew more warmth from playing the piano for the Revelly's as they danced together. Again, when every night Elizabeth read her the bible, the messages and meaning captivated her. Last of all, in accordance with Emily's wishes, Henry was left in the care of a loving free colonists family. Thus emerged was a deep Christian, believer of hope, courageous, playful, and growing intelligent free lady.

CHAPTER 21

It is late 1790.

The now 15-year-old Emily Wilson laid across a bulky gum tree branch. Her bare feet lazily swayed in the air weightlessly. She was too exhausted to dream past the leafy shade. Instead, she listened to the voices of the colony's movement and surrounding nature.

Turning her gaze, Emily sat upright. A tall, handsome, lanky, and thin railed convict gazed intently back at her. But there was more to the gaze when Emily locked eyes with him. There was understanding in their fate. He seemed to read her convict past like a weightless book. It was like their convictions had effortlessly entwined. It was like that sharp entwining blossomed understanding between their numb minds. But it brought a sharp surge of pain in their fast beating hearts. It was that pain that blossomed into developing love. Kindling love that brought the convict man before her.

"Good day me lady," greeted the man with a slight bow of his head.

"Good day as well. Name?" Emily slipped her hands into his. She let his strong arms, hardened by labour, lift her down. She even allowed him to hold her close.

"Abraham. You?"

"Emily Wilson," blushed Emily.

"What a lovely name."

"Yes indeed."

Silence followed, soon lifted by Abraham inquiring, "Are you one of us?"

Emily glanced at his dirty and patched clothes. HIs long-sleeved white and black striped shirt was too long and big for his frame. He wore a faded red scarf around his pale neck. He wore long white pants that fell to his bony ankles. Chains bound his ankles, so he may not take flight. He wore black leather shoes and a black convict cap[5].

He wore an unbuttoned brown jacket that was too long for his frame. Emily glanced back, his blue eyes bore the weight of his conviction and burning love for her. She felt the scars in his worn hands. She stroked his chin, his complexion darkened by the days spent labouring under the hot Australian sun. She removed his convict cap. She ran her fingers through his greasy, oily, and sweaty short silky black hair.

---

[5] The convict cap was made from leather. It consisted of two flaps tied together that dropped down to form a brim. These caps are known as the convict hats. It was given to convicts from 1820 to 1855 by the British government. However, prior to 1820 there were convicts who wore this headdress.

"Yes," sighed Emily at last.

Abraham showed hardly any recognition. He slid a finger under her chin and gently lifted it up. She slipped her arms around his neck. Closing their eyes, their lips felt each other. Bestow true love and understanding at the first site.

CHAPTER 22

Emily stood outside the boundaries of the men's tents. Her fingers wrapped around a thin wooden post. Her heart beat fast in longing to see Abraham. In hungry yearning, she cried to be with him. The sun weakly rose behind the tents, capturing the shelters in a shade of orange-purple shadow. The ringing of a bell to announce 6am made her jump. The lighting of lamps and candles danced shadows in the shelters. Slurred voices announced movement.

Keeping low, Emily moved to the left. She caught the glimpse of men, dressed in a similar manner to Abraham, huddling before a group of marines and guards. Thin-railed, gnawing from starvation, sick, and shriving from the early cold; Emily felt a wave of understanding. She felt it strengthened her soul to know she could intellectually feel this connection with these poor souls. She was too far to hear the voices, the smugly dressed overseers conducted the roll call.

Straining her ears, the booming voices projected the individual names of the convict men and boys. Barely did she hear the gruffled replies. The jingling and snapping of the ankle chains revived her chain bound memories. Her ears perked at feet shuffling towards the wooden posts. Shrinking further back, her vision saw a large line of convicts accompanied by their overseers and marines march forward.

Those severely sick or injured still remained huddled as they waited to report. Taking a deep breath, Emily slithered through. The gruff surprises were quickly silenced by their overseers. When the last men had filed out, Emily heard the last footfalls echo in the distance. She dared not breathe again until she sighted no figures. Turning her gaze, she was greeted by an array of tents lined neatly in rows.

Her feet fell lightly against the terrain as she walked down the paths. The light wind stirred the flyers of the tents. That stir brought a dreary eeriness to her eardrums. It ignited, then tickled that sensation inside her. Then it brought a surge of curiosity that glided her forward.

Entering a tent, her vision discerned the shape of objects in the dimness. She picked out a low and flimsy stretcher. She instantly knew the occupant was a convict themselves. The frailed thin blankets confirmed their status. The edge of a mouldy and colouring portrait in the dust, caught the corner of her eyes. Picking it up, she blew the dust away to reveal a portrait of a woman.

The beauty and grace in her manners pained the girl's heart. The radiation of life drew her trauma and worries for a mother she had been ripped from. It brought her tears to think that, just like this lonely convict, she would never again see the faces of her beloved native family. Thus she felt the tickle of grieved tears leak for them.

At last, she shook her head and laid the picture on the blankets. Taking a deep breath, she shakily wiped her eyes. Emerging into the sunlight, she stole one last glance behind her. Then, something caught her attention.

There was a flash of human flesh down the path. Lightly down the path she skipped. The clanging of a dragging chain guided her poor sense of direction. She stopped, and dared not to breathe. Chilly wind brushed past her. Suddenly she felt colder. She tightly clutched her pale green shawl around her chilled neck. Her breath frosted the once humid air. She closed her eyes. Her physique shook in response to the coldness. The laying of a hand on her shoulder snapped her vision to attention. Behold, was a spiritual ghost.

Examining closely, she gasped. They had once been one of her clan, a convict. They had been ripped from homeland, family, identity, and life. They had been convicted for either stealing to survive, or for practising the wrongest of crimes. But when she saw how malnourished their physique was, she knew the battle for survival had been to no avail. It even cringed her to see the damned chains laden their bony ankles. Their ill-fitted and frailed clothes, along with their dishevelled features, confirmed their conviction.

They locked eyes. His emptiness brought tears of grief to her frightened ones. Hanging her head, the man watched the tears stain her pale cheeks. Slipping a finger under her chin, his hands wiped her eyes. But those hands did more than erasing the emerging grief and pain. It melted comfort into her despair. Comfort, that warmed her shaking body and poured it with new strength.

The figure nodded their head in understanding. A blankness then dazed his still expression. He moved away, coldness returning to her. Confused by his motives, Emily cried. Her voice weakly called for his return. Halting, they stretched their shrunken hands in gesture. A gesture that was taken with shaking hands.

And with every step, hands entwined, she felt connection in this dreary place. The eeriness breathed alive the presences, the stories, and sufferings, of these individuals in her soul. It stung her heart and sparked her curiosity. That spark drew her strength to continue forward with the spiritual ghost. The ghosts' mythical presence aroused a fluster of conjured voices that filtered from the tents. They voiced their stories and future hopes.

At last, it became too much and she closed her hearing to those hushes. For she fights to largely forget her past, and only remember her unravelling future. A future that she had no time to ponder upon, having entered an officer's tent. Releasing her hand, the mythical man bowed his head. Nodding in return, she made to examine the interior. With the entrance having been tied back, she welcomed the glow of the sunlight. The spiritual ghost stood observing nearby.

In the beautifully smooth and crafted wooden drawers, she saw an array of civilian and military clothing. Having closed them, she was arrested by the display of portraits of women and children. Sharply drawing her attention away, she smiled at a hammock slightly swaying in the filtering wind. Exhaustion filled her soul as she fell into its smoothness. She nestled and curled into a protective ball.

Hiding in the officer's hammock, Emily felt the smoothness of the heavy fabric. Most of all, she felt a deep connection and understanding to the convicts of these tents. For, in her old childhood, she had experienced the hell, suffering, that broke a convict down. She may have not experienced the construction labour under the boiling sun, but she had suffered abuse, exploitation, and the grin of house labour. She had suffered an unconsented marriage and forced sexual intercourse.

She had experienced 6am awakenings like them. She had been beaten, punished, and flogged like these men and boys. She had seen felons suffer from starvation, dehydration, heat, coldness, racking coughs, injuries, and severe illness. She had endured the horrifying journey in the ships to a land many seas away. She had lost loved ones and witnessed felons perish. She had seen mates brutally slaughtered or punished.

She had been severely weakened and deprived of sunlight like them. She had been deprived of her human freedoms and rights like them. She had been deprived of her dignity and self-identity like them. And like several other children, convicted for the pettiest crime in their struggle for survival, she had lost her childhood. But she had commenced her new childhood in loving arms.

She had met her first and only true love. Now, she was desperate to see that love.

Unknown to her, the spiritual ghost had been nothing but a comforting conjure of her stung trauma. So when Emily was startled at footsteps falling beside her, the ghost had gone. Her daze was pulled together by the sight of James kneeling nearby. "We are all looking for you all over the cove."

"I'm sorry," Emily stood to her feet with her head bowed.

"You don't know any better. You have lost yourself in the hell you have so bravely endured for too long," defended James. Slipping a finger under her chin, James lifted the girl's head up and tenderly kissed her forehead.

"And it's a miracle I'm still alive," sniffled Emily.

"Yes."

"Found her?" one of the earlier figures entered. He appeared to be a guard of some sort.

"Yes, but I want to make sure nothing horrible happened to her," James confirmed.

"None of the men knew of my entrance. They were going out to what I suspect as labour," confirmed Emily.

"So you snuck in?" a kindle of pride warmed James' voice.

"Yes," sheepishly answered Emily.

"She ought to be flogged!" exclaimed the guard.

"No, she has already been flogged. Elizabeth and I will discuss the matter alone with her," James asserted.

James guided Emily out, the guard nearby. Upon exiting the tent area, Elizabeth rejoiced.

"My dear, what a silent mouse you are! Slipping away without our knowledge tells me how cheeky you are. You frightened my poor old heart when I found empty blankets this morning," Elizabeth hugged Emily close and tenderly kissed the girl's forehead several times. Emily murmured in remorse, tightly clutching the lady's sleeves.

"Come now, we have matters to discuss," beckoned James.

"Why did you depart without telling us so?" Elizabeth inquired. Her vision watched the girl stare at her tucker. The puffing of smoke nearby singled James' presence.

"I met a man yesterday by the name of Abraham. He's an iron chain felon like me myself once. His appearance confirmed his place in society. Thus I felt this deep surge of remorse, understanding, and pain like he did. Then, we felt love for one another. Thus we touched and kissed," Emily clutched Elizabeth's hand. The girl's eyes gazed in the distance. Her complexion blushed.

"Emily, my dear. You have fallen in love at first sight. I only suspect it through your actions with him. What did the kiss feel like?" Elizabeth saw a smile crack to the girl's lips.

"Real love," Emily dreamily stated.

"Then, it's real and true love," confirmed Elizabeth.

Emily eagerly turned to the lady, but a grave realisation consumed her excitement. "I can't marry him. I ain't any virgin, and still a convict under yer care." Tears choked the girl's throat.

"My dear, if you inform him of your past with Jackson, then the understanding between you two will strengthen. You hadn't agreed to it, so may Abraham know of it if he intends on having children with you. Pain shadows the past. It refrains us from discussing it. But without sharing the burden, then the past shall never feel lighter. Abraham and you share similar pasts, so may it be most understood between you two. Thus be sure to share the burden with Abraham. As for marriage, your positions in society can never hold your burning love for one another apart. With our positions in society, I am sure we can gain Phillip's approval for a marriage between you two."

"Yes, I know Abraham and I can share the burden of our pasts," Emily closed her eyes. "But mine is slightly different to his. Yet I feel he's gonna understand the most. Thus I gotta have this burden shared with him as you say."

"That's right," agreed Elizabeth with a thoughtful nod.

Opening her eyes, Emily sighed, "I can't leave you two through. You both are the only comforting kin left to me."

"Then Abraham and you can live with us," reassured Elizabeth.

"Oh, thank you!" joyfully cried Emily.

Silence fell, soon lifted by Elizabeth stating, "You are too young to marry through. Wait until you're seventeen. My own mother wouldn't let me experience marriage nor sex until then.

"Yes, I suppose," submitted Emily with a smile.

CHAPTER 23

She had lost. She had suffered. She had won. Now, the search for her internal self had begun. She had begun to prick past her wound of tumour to revisit her memories. Memories that stored her past self and the life she had endured. And with closed eyes, she could see it herself.

She could see her beloved father. She could sense his weakness, as the blankets wrapped him. She could feel the hollowness of his hands, held gently by his wife and daughter. She cried at the strength of love that surrounded him in his last breath. She could feel the renewed pain, then the grief that had accompanied their hearts.

She had sensed the Lord's welcoming of his spirit to Heaven. She could sense the loss as they reunited with her grandma; their few precious possessions following them. The bleak buildings of London, and its smoky sky, she could feel its dampness. Those cobbled streets of poverty; the innocent she had witnessed perished. She had become like those children; ridden by poorness, displaced by endless suffering, and lost within themselves.

Thus, on a spree they went, stealing the wealthy's nourishment to feed their crying families. Then Emily had paid the price; facing goal, conviction, and transportation to exile. And in that she had lost her childhood, and the arms of motherly comfort. Now the endless salty waves, that crashed against the sandy cove shores, separated daughter and mother.

Thus, whenever she met Abraham's eyes, she was reminded of the losses of her mother and father. For he bought back the pain and the grief of those years. Those empty eyes, his skinny hollowness; it enshrined a reflection of her past. How she longed, fought for that forgottenness. But how it only made her soul, developing love, cry for him. Yet, his sufferings gave her strength to find herself. It ignited the hope of Abraham finding the light to find himself.

For diseases and starvation had driven him to fight for his life through thief. Now, her search for herself drove him to find his internal self. Exiled as a convict, to this far flung colony of hell Abraham was. For what? Losing his beloved kin to diseases? Fighting for his life? Even if it meant stealing the nourishment from his wealthier counterparts. Wasn't it better to have been hung in his homeland, then face the hell of this hot, dusty, and dry colony?

For a lack of sufficient nourishment kept their bodies starving here. How could they even seek the littlest humane compassion? Why did they have to defect, die from the suffering, commit suicide, or harm others to gain even the slightest of it? It was useless, for their fallen lives were only mildly thought off. Yet, Abraham felt the Lord had spoken to him.

He grasped the last of his fledging hope and held onto its will. For he had believed in a future. He had believed in comfort and love, when all around him fell. The comfort, the love, is now in Emily alone. Yet, after Jackson's brutality, he had sensed her hesitation in romance. But he knew he had to seek her love and show his. For her voice, her body, her laughter; he alone responded. Never would he now respond to the marines or overseers. And he was just like her. He had a name, a deceased Irish family, a life, and a meaning.

CHAPTER 24

Freedom he had been born in, but conviction had kidnapped it. Goal, transportation, suffering, hell, and chains had shackled them all. It had deprived them of their names, of their beloved kins, of their homelands, and of internal meaning. For the Lord may have forgiven them, but their rulers hadn't.

Convicts and worthless dirt they were. Abraham is one of them. Emily once had been one of them. For he had suffered the grief of loss. He had stood hopeless; diseases slaughtering his poor Irish family. The grief had renewed; as his hands moved the soil over their cold and unmoving bodies.

Then he had been forced to steal the nourishment. Young, yet wasting on the streets of poverty. Stealing from the wealthy; devouring their nourishment. Then caught he was, and thrown into goal's depths. Then across the channel to the land of the British, to their hell of NewGate Prison, he was transferred. But his truest battle had only commenced with the broading of the First Fleet and their human cargo. And part of that cargo he was. Then his life, vision, had changed with the meeting of his love. Thus, the desperate battle to secure one another had only commenced.

CHAPTER 25

It was another one of those beautiful Australian spring days. Elizabeth and James were out for the day, so they had disposed of the unusually quiet girl in Surgeon White's care. And indeed Emily needed quietness. She was strained by the burden of her past, that bestowed shame and mixed tumbling emotions. On Top of that, her true love conflicted with that burden.

She was able to share a convict's burden with Abraham, whose convictions understood it all. Yet, she felt the loss of virginity in Jackson's exploitation of her had disappointed Abraham. Little did she know, Abraham spent endless nights of harrowing worry over her traumatised marriage. Even her life before that marriage, and Jackson's cold blooded slaughter of her Irish mates, emotionally tormented him. Despite it all, despite her hesitation around showing him her love, Abraham knew their burning unconditional love for each other bounded them more than anything.

He knew they would have each other, close, not separated in two worlds apart, after their sentences. But it wrenched them. Emily would desperately spend many nights secretly visiting Abraham. Abraham, who became so desperate for her presence, would escape the tents to be with her nightly. But convicts' secrets are always sniffed out by the bored marines.

Emily knew the marines must have sniffed it out when he didn't come one night. So distressed she was, Emily ran to Elizabeth pleading to be allowed out to locate Abraham. Not even the alarmed Elizabeth's reassurances could coax the hysterical girl to slumber.

Elizabeth's worry grew with every stubborn and firm refusal to obey the routine and order from a bleary eyed Emily. So the lady had urgently called on the good surgeon to explain the situation. He warmly agreed to care for Emily while the Revelly's spent time together. However, even his warm tone couldn't bring forward a nerve frayed girl. For, she was trapped in a strong well of misery and worry. He instead allowed the silent sombre girl to shelter herself in the shadow by the tent hospital entrance.

There, she heard the echoes of a helpless soul as they were being flogged. Sprinting to her feet, Emily strained her ears and clutched her fast beating heart. She couldn't be mistaken; those strangled, pained, masculine cries belonged to her beloved Abraham. She sprinted to her feet and ran towards the suffering. Surgeon White sprung after her.

Her enraged anger over the flogging of her beloved man drained the surgeon's protests. Reaching the site, Emily's complexion drained off all colour. Abraham screamed in strangled cries and buckled with each flog. The dark blood gushed from his damaged tissue and soaked his back flesh. The blood dripped onto the orangeish dirt, staining its complexion.

He knew the pain, the shame that every lashing bestowed, must be endured. Thus struggle did he not, but the roaring of his vocal did he allow. And with every roar, every flog, a new wave of powerful boiling anger filled Emily.

"NO!" screamed Emily, running towards the ferrule bearer.

"Stop her!" ordered the officer.

"Let him go!" roared Emily. She struggled as the marine wrapped an arm around her waist. His iron grip rubbed against her hip bone. Other marines hurried forward, gripping her arms, legs, knees, and ankles. Another clamped a sweaty hand over her mouth.

Emily squirmed, as they fastened their grips. She tried lashing out, but the pain depleted her strength.

"Let go of the girl!" demanded Surgeon White. Breathless, he hunched over before the marines. "I can calm her. Please, just go and get the Revelly's here quickly. They are having tea at the beach with some ladies and their husbands."

His order was heeded, the marines released the girl and hurried away.

"No, don't calm me down!" raged Emily. Tears blurred her vision.

"Listen to me! Listen to me now!" demanded the surgeon. He swooped in and grasped her ankles.

"I won't, I won't!" Emily violently kicked until she had loosened his grip. But the surgeon had wrapped his arm tightly around her waist.

"There is nothing you can do for Abraham!"

"No, I can stop them!

"Take her away!" ordered the officer angrily. Surgeon White failed to hear, his eardrums deafened by her hysterical fits. Leaning in closer, the officer, "Now!"

"Emily!" cried Elizabeth, James at her heel. Grabbing her legs, James assisted the surgeon to carry the struggling girl out.

Emily fought and fought, until she had dislodged their grasps. Elizabeth grabbed her arm and pulled. Emily tried pulling against her strong grasp, but strength wouldn't prevail against the girl. But Emily pushed her exhaustion until her fingers firmly wrapped around the wooden boundary surrounding the flogging pole.

"Stop hurting him!" screamed Emily. The angry blue coated man quickly approached her.

"Emily, come back now!" screamed Elizabeth, frantically pulling. But it was to no avail, for the man tore them apart. He punched the air from Emily's lungs. His hand slapped her face several times, blurring Emily's vision. James angrily thrust him away. Collapsing, Emily wailed and curled into a protective ball. Whimpering, her hands shakily shielded her face. Elizabeth fell to her knees and protectively held the girl close.

"Back off!" growled James. His eyes burned in flames of anger. Anger, that ignited fear in the abuser. Shakily holding his hands before him, the man backed away without uttering another word.

CHAPTER 26

It is now 1812. 35-year-old Emily Wilson stood under the shade of a gumtree. She wistfully gazed at a figure balanced on a shiny, fit, and strong black stallion.

Since 17-years-of age, Emily has been bound to her beloved Abraham through marriage. Abraham, who shared the relief of the birth of their beloved daughter. Relife, that turned into the strongest of love for their screaming and wailing newborn. It made her think of her deceased mother and grandmother in Heaven. Her heart leaked for them, but she silently knew they felt her joys through the internals of Heaven. She knew that their starved souls forever watched over her.

For they had watched the unconditional love of Elizabeth and James rear the lifeable, beautiful girl into a world of convicts, marines, settlers, and officers. A world that Emily wanted her daughter, a spitting image of her mother, to forge a better life in. She doesn't want her to bear the burden of her convict's parents' past. She doesn't want her to bear the shame and humiliation the title brings them. The emotional toil from it had broken them down.

The girl had sensed her parents' wish for their only child. She may not have understood the scars of their lives, but she sensed the emotional turmoil of it. Thus the girl, now an 18-year-old woman, took it upon herself to bring glory to the Wilson title. And she knew as a woman, it would prove even harder. But the determination gave her will and meaning to strike out the path to glory alone. And now that day has arrived.

Now, Emily had to temporarily farewell her daughter for as long as the journey took. Emily had sensed the day's arrival. She felt it from the moment she first locked eyes with her newborn. She felt it from the radiation of her strong character. But seeing her only child go into a largely unexplored bush alone, brought her much emotion. The pride warmed her heart, but made her realise just how much she truly loved her daughter. Love, that has brought her worry since the child learnt their first steps.

Now, the worry burdened her more. What if the Aboriginals killed her daughter out of prejudice? What if starvation, dehydration, heat, cold, injuries, and illness bowed her down withering to the hard clay terrain? But closing her vision and breathing cleared those worries away. Her daughter will survive all the hardships in the forged shield of determination, unconditional love, courage, and will.

The memories of her child brought her fiery love. Fiery love, that formed the deepest of bonds of enduring love and courage to face the months long separation. Separation, that would see her daughter's waltzing of the to be beloved bush. A bush, full of the harshest of hardships that is waiting like a gem to be explored and endured. A bush that stole the heart of Australia's first white native born generation. A bush that called the child to a place of truest glory.

A glory that her daughter itched to explore. And as her daughter galloped into the unknown with a crack of the whip, Emily allowed the shield to strengthen her soul. She knew, deep down, her daughter would not only bring glory to the Wilson title, but come back to the loving arms of her childhood.

www.ingramcontent.com/pod-product-compliance
Lightning Source LLC
Chambersburg PA
CBHW061106100726
47911CB00012B/427